The Last Ditch

K.M. PEYTON

The Last Ditch

OXFORD UNIVERSITY PRESS

Oxford   Toronto   Melbourne

Oxford University Press, Walton Street, Oxford OX2 6DP
Oxford London Glasgow
New York Toronto Melbourne Auckland
Kuala Lumpur Singapore Hong Kong Tokyo
Delhi Bombay Calcutta Madras Karachi
Nairobi Dar es Salaam Cape Town

and associated companies in
Beirut Berlin Ibadan Mexico City Nicosia

Oxford is a trade mark of Oxford University Press

Peyton, K.M.
The last ditch.
I. Title
823'.914[J]   PZ7
ISBN 0-19-271484-8

Typeset by Tradespools Limited, Frome, Somerset
Printed and bound in Great Britain by
Biddles Ltd, Guildford and King's Lynn

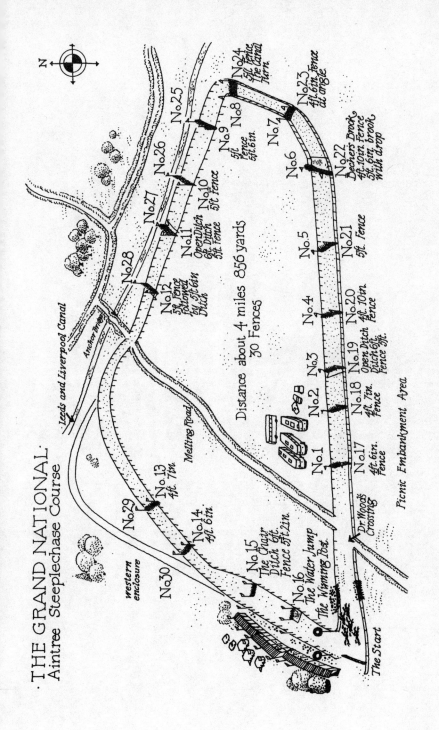

THE GRAND NATIONAL.
Aintree Steeplechase Course

Chapter 1

Even while it was actually happening, Jonathan kept thinking: it can't be true ... it's just like a Martini advertisement ... lying on the beach in the swooning Greek sunshine, seeing the girl coming towards him out of the water, her long blonde hair falling loose over thin brown shoulders, dropping down beside him....

'I do love you so, Jonathan. Will you make love to me?' Kissing him, stroking his hair. Holy Cow!

'They won't be back for hours. They've gone fishing,' she said.

He wanted to say, 'But I don't love you,' but people in advertisements never said that, and it was unkind. It seemed to matter somehow, but nobody else would agree; he was an idiot to think so. He could not think of a single person he knew who would think it mattered. Her hair was smothering him. He rolled over and propped himself up on one elbow.

'Steady on,' he said.

'I'm not a horse.' She sounded indignant, quite rightly.

'No ... sorry—'

'Won't you?'

'I—'

'It will never be like this again.'

'No.' Funny, but he had been thinking that before she came, without sex coming into it. He had been thinking that this place, Sivota on Levkas, wasn't half bad and to be visiting it on a private yacht was pretty plushy too, when half his age-group was on the dole, and he had been wondering what he had done to deserve his enviable lot and whether it was bad for one's nature to have life so easy and parents so rich and luxuries so commonplace ... to have the girl actually offering herself as well was ludicrous. I shall suffer for it later, he thought, when I'm old. He was a great one for guilt complexes.

'I know you don't love me,' she said helpfully. 'Don't feel bad about it. I know what I'm doing. I just want you—now. No strings attached.'

She smiled down at him, her face shaded by the curtains of her hair. She was a green and gold girl, beautiful when the conditions were right, too thin, too intense, nutty as a fruitcake. They were in the Sixth form together at one of Britain's most exclusive schools. Her mother was a famous cello player who was never at home and Iris found homes where she could, presently with Jonathan's family. Jonathan tended to avoid her if he could, but being pathetically kind by nature, he was not very successful.

He did not say anything, not wanting to give anything away, nervous as hell after the first shock. She started kissing him again. After a bit she said, 'I know a place, up the hill. No one will come, and it's beautiful. Will you, Jonathan?'

By now he was not averse, the idea having taken hold. One did not have to be intellectual about these things. He climbed up the goat-track behind her, slightly more breathless than the hill demanded. He never had before; had she? Not properly, that is. It was just another of life's blessings, that the first time was to be celebrated on a Mediterranean hillside with the sort of view that had prompted Byron, Shelley, Keats, etc. to timeless verse—the normal grope on the back seat of a borrowed car was obviously for lesser mortals. Me and Byron, Jonathan thought, sought after by women ... he felt slightly stoned, his pleasure senses sharpened by shock and delight, responsibility dulled. With him it was usually the other way round. Could it really be as easy, as beautiful, as this?

Yes, well, it was.

He still could not believe it.

Why, at home, was everything so complicated? It could never be like this at home, in Britain. The ground would be cold for a start and one would have a whole lot of clothes to take off. Here the ground was warm and smelled of honey, and they were virtually naked anyway. They were securely alone, no sound of traffic, tractors, jumbo jets, only a distant cracked goat-bell and the humming of occasional insects. Through the silvery olive-leaves the sun glittered and swung above, and below the azure sea washed the white shining rocks where the flowers and the trees gave way to the shore. There was a track scarred into the hillside that led to a tiny hut on the shore round the next headland, the M1 of this magical nowhere; and through the haze out at sea the slumbering outline of Ithaca, and Cephalonia beyond, rose like a mirage, trembling in the heat. The heat, away from the water, was intense. It washed over their sated bodies as they lay in this amazing state of indolent bliss, stunning conscience.

Iris slept and Jonathan lay watching the incredible sea through his eyelashes, thinking about things, until the triangular white sail of a yacht 'Martha Mooney' inched round the headland, scarcely filling, heading for home. On the yacht were his mother and father, his sister, his uncle Jeremy, his auntie Sarah and his cousins, Charles and Amy. Jonathan sighed.

Iris woke up and said how much she loved him. Jonathan wished she wouldn't; it made him feel bad about the whole thing. He could not bring himself to say it when he didn't. She was altogether too airy-fairy for his taste. He liked steady, quiet girls with enigmatic smiles. Iris was given to hysterical joys and intense glooms which tended to devour her companions at the time. Not a man to reveal his feelings overmuch, Jonathan was made profoundly uneasy by her excesses, but his mother, a hard, horsey woman whom he also found hard to live with, seemed to enjoy her company and asked her home for the holidays when Jonathan would rather have let the whole thing

3

drop. His mother said he was very intolerant, but Jonathan thought he was quite the opposite; they never agreed about much, him and his mother. His mother was always wanting him to have 'nice friends' but Jonathan did not go looking for friends. In his experience they tended to disappear or get killed just when you were getting to depend on them. Peter McNair was away now, with a job in National Hunt racing, and Jonathan supposed that was another one gone, the one he would least have had depart.

'When you get to Oxford,' his mother said, 'you'll meet plenty of congenial boys and girls.'

Puke, thought Jonathan.

He did not want to go to Oxford either.

But then he opened his eyes wide and remembered what had happened and saw how very all right this place was and stopped bothering. He got up and went back down the track with Iris, holding her hand. Half-way down he stopped and kissed her again, in gratitude really, and she said, 'You mustn't worry about not loving me. I don't mind—I mean, I would rather you did, but I see how it is, and it doesn't matter.'

'I don't want to make you miserable,' he said.

'No. You won't. Not if you carry on like this.'

That worried him rather, but they walked on down to the taverna on the shore and sat down at a table under the vines to wait until the yacht had anchored. Sivota—a mere collection of stone cottages and two tavernas miles from anywhere—commanded a land-locked bay completely sheltered from the open sea, the entry being under wooded cliffs between two headlands. It was popular with yachts, but only one or two were anchored there now. Martha, when she appeared, ghosting under the pines, had plenty of room to round up. They watched Uncle Jeremy supervising the manouevre, Jessica and Charles squabbling as to who should let down the mainsail, Jonathan's father releasing the anchor. Jonathan liked his family better at a distance, over a glass of ouzo. (The waiter had brought them ouzo and a jug of water, and Jonathan, wearing only swimming trunks, had promised to pay him later.) They were making frightfully British conversation in clear, carrying voices. What had the Greeks done to deserve them? Jonathan wondered, disapproving strongly of tourism and what it had done to places, even while enjoying being a tourist no end, ouzo and all. One was incredibly arrogant abroad. He would never have dreamed of going into a strange restaurant at home in his swimming trunks and having a drink without any money to pay for it, yet it seemed quite natural here.

Perhaps he wouldn't have dreamed of getting involved with Iris either: a nice euphemism, 'getting involved', but it could hardly be called making love, when love was not involved. Why did the fact worry him so? He supposed because he knew that, by accepting the invitation, he was now in part committed. Iris was no joker, having sex for fun; Iris was a dramatic, highly-emotional, love-starved female, not averse to flinging herself in rivers when crossed. The euphemism for this was 'a cry for help' and, since he had helped, Iris had loved him.

'Look, Iris,' he said, feeling compelled, 'I don't want you to think ... I mean, it was wrong, I shouldn't have, when I don't—' He paused.

'Love me?'

'Mmm.'

'But you've already said. I accept it. It needn't worry you.'

'I can't help it.'

Another, more practical, thought struck him. 'I say, I never thought—I never used a—'

'Oh, really, Jonathan, I hardly expected you to have one on you, dressed like that! You needn't worry. I'm on the pill.'

Jonathan found he was blushing scarlet. Her news amazed him. Had she planned his seduction? He had always thought a girl had to start on the pill three months

5

or so in advance for it to be any good. Perhaps he had it wrong. He wasn't being at all the suave lover he had always hoped he would prove; Iris was laughing at him. Bloody hell. This is what came of having scruples. Old-fashioned scruples at that. He stood up rather abruptly and said, 'We'd better go back.'

'We'll do it again,' she said, smiling. 'You can't say you didn't enjoy it?'

'I'll go and fetch the dinghy for you.'

He turned and dived so rapidly off the quay he nearly clobbered himself on a mooring post and had to twist ferociously on surfacing to avoid decapitation.

Iris, left alone, found she was trembling, and drank her ouzo rapidly, hoping intoxication might make her feel better. She had done it, screwed up her courage at last to experience this thing that Jane and them at school were forever rabbiting on about, cornered Jonathan so that he had had no escape, forced him ... but the effort to appear blasé about the whole business had left her close to total collapse. Her teeth chattered on the glass. It was true that she had wanted it, and known that only by making the advance herself was it ever likely to happen, for Jonathan was not a natural flirt, even had he loved her, which she knew perfectly well he didn't. And although she loved him desperately, she had always been content with her romantic, one-sided adoration: she had not wished its consummation in the way Jane and them were always discussing, save for one reason. She choked over the aniseed strength of her ouzo, still shivering. What an idiot she was! Always doing the wrong thing, saying tactless truths, drowning in her own gauche inadequacy. But she had determined to get Jonathan to make love to her; she had been successful. Her drink should be a celebration, not medicinal alcohol to combat complete disintegration. And it was no good weakening. The relationship had to be pursued farther for her plan to be successful and anyone but her idiot self would be contemplating the next step with eager anticipation. Well, perhaps when the shock-waves had receded, she would. After all, a girl was deflowered only once in a lifetime and it was not an act to be taken lightly, even at the advanced age of eighteen. Not by her, at least.

The panics receded, the heady drink lulling her. What a seductive place this was! The distant tinkling of goat-bells up on the opposite shore was the only sound, broken presently by the slow splash of oars breaking the water as Jonathan came back. Iris, used to loneliness, would have preferred to be alone for a bit now, to get used to her new status in life, but there was no chance. She had to keep up her front before Jonathan. His face was now wary in the way she knew so well. One did not easily take liberties with Jonathan; he was an essentially private sort of person. But he smiled, and she was comforted.

'I've got the money for the drinks. If you leave it on the table—'

He handed it up. She put it with the empty glasses, and stepped down into the dinghy.

'They wanted to know what we'd been doing while they were away,' he said.

'What did you say?'

'I said studying biology up on the cliffs. They assumed I meant flowers.'

Iris laughed then. He was lovely, in spite of what Jane said. Jane said he was 'positively mediaeval', which Iris took to mean old-fashioned, probably because he had ignored Jane's usual invitations; she said he was 'dreadfully stuffy' because her jokes did not amuse him and 'a real creep of the establishment' because he had been made Head Prefect. But she had never denied his physical attractiveness, and no one was more practised at making judgements on male allure than Jane. He had a hard, athletic body with a hint still of the endearing gawkiness of adolescence. Not a one for public school games, he was fit

7

with mountaineering and riding, and he didn't smoke like most of them. ('Biggles', Jane called him when she was being really bitchy). His natural expression was serious, with a hint of cautiousness, yet he was not cautious by inclination. He had springy black hair which was apt to run riot into a mass of positive ringlets after swimming or when neglected and which Iris knew was a source of great irritation to him. All the same, it was not cut particularly short.

'They've only come back for us,' he said. 'We're off to somewhere for a meal.'

'Where?'

'They're all arguing. Vassiliki or Nidri or Spatahori.'

'The food's all the same wherever you go.'

'Yes. The taverna here is as good as any.'

Iris steeled herself to go back into company, the full weight of Jonathan's family in close confinement being definitely overpowering. His mother and father and his uncle Jeremy were all what might be termed 'natural leaders of men'; auntie Sarah was blessedly acquiescent, but the other three young were noisy and tedious. Jonathan's sister Jessica, aged sixteen, considered herself in love with a boy at home and hadn't wanted to come, so quarrelled and sulked intermittently; Charles and Amy at sixteen and fourteen were boisterous and tried to make Iris go wind-surfing, which terrified her. Iris found it hard to adapt, having been a solitary child for seventeen years. Since she had gone home with Jonathan last summer, when her mother had neglected to make any arrangements for her, she had followed the pattern in subsequent holidays, finding Jonathan's home life very congenial. Mrs Meredith, his renowned 'awful' mother, had welcomed her and the invitations had been made on her part, not by Jonathan. Whether Jonathan welcomed them or resented them Iris had never known. Their house was big enough for him to avoid her if he chose and certainly he had never behaved towards her in anything but a brotherly fashion.

8

Until today.

Shipping an oar to come alongside, he now gave a smile, 'Back to barracks. Report for duty.'

But the family was tired after its day's fishing and in a pleasantly harmonious mood, the adults lolling about with gin and tonics.

'You two have been doing nothing all day. Sail us to—where are we going?'

'Nidri.'

'Vassiliki.'

'Spatahori.'

'Fine. Skipper can choose then. Wherever you like. Jonathan.'

Jonathan shrugged, smiled. Iris felt deeply worried, as always when situations of responsibility hove on the immediate horizon but Jonathan said, amazingly, 'You can join the gin party, if you like. I'll do it.'

'On your own?'

'You'd have to be very clever indeed to wreck a boat on a day like this, even on your own,' he said.

It was true, she supposed, but the mystique of sailing—as she felt it to be—disturbed her deeply: even to the clever names for every bit of rope and every edge of sail, the incomprehensible orders to the helm, luff up, bear away, point higher, free off—she hadn't cottoned on to a word of it, even after a fortnight. It had taken her a whole week to realize that the sheets they talked about were not the actual sails but the bits of rope on their tail-ends that had to be made fast, winched in, eased off or let fly as the case may be, for what actual reason she would never know. She sat down feeling very useless and watched Jonathan methodically set about getting the boat under way alone, taking off the sail tiers, checking the halyards were free, pulling in the kedge. In the deeply sheltered inlet the wind was very fluky and unreliable, but the family liked to handle the boat under sail as a point of honour, and only used the engine if absolutely necessary, or in very crowded moorings. They were those sort of people, Iris recognized, not given to easy options, even on holiday. And although the adults were now apparently talking about house prices and capital gains tax she knew perfectly well that they were acutely aware of whether Jonathan was doing the job properly or not, and she knew that Jonathan was acutely aware that he was under scrutiny: that was the awful thing about his family, this compulsion to do everything as well as possible and the impossibly high standards they set themselves, even in the things they did for fun, not just A-level results and making another million before the New Year. (Both she and Jonathan would have their A-level results waiting when they got home, but that was something she preferred not to think about). She supposed that Jonathan, having been brought up in this way, would live to perpetrate it on a family of his own when he was adult, just as she, brought up by a hopelessly irresponsible mother, would never learn sense herself.

'Will you have a drink, Iris?' kindly Aunt Sarah asked, the only one who would not mind if Jonathan sailed them into the bar of the taverna (it had been known).

'No, not gin, thank you.'

'Just tonic? There's ice still, and lemon.'

'Yes, very well. But don't get up. I'll do it.'

Jonathan stepped over her to put a sheet round the winch. The big yacht was moving, idly it seemed, but the olive grove on the far beach was coming up fast. He hauled the sheet in and made it fast and moved across to the wheel. He moved as fast as he could without looking as if he was in a hurry. Nobody moved a muscle to help but they were all watching like hawks and the subject of capital gains was losing impetus—unlike the yacht. Iris felt the panics rising. The yacht heeled suddenly as a fluky gust caught her and bolted for the nearest pile of rocks with a roar of water under her bow. Jonathan spun the wheel, leapt across to free the sheet he had just made fast. Iris was sitting on the loose coils and squealed as they galvanized into life under her bare flesh.

'Move!' Jonathan hissed, and was leaping across to the starboard sheet without any pretence at all to nonchalance. The winch grated noisily, the yacht came upright in her tracks and spun round on her heel as gracefully as a ballet-dancer. Jonathan skipped back to the wheel and checked it and the yacht paid off away from the shore with a sweet chuckling of her bow-wave, and Uncle Jeremy said, 'They're the very devil, these winds off steep shores. You never know what to expect. Is there any more tonic, Sarah?'

'I'll open another bottle. Perhaps Jonathan would like a drink?'

Uncle Jeremy said, 'No, keep him sober till we're out. This is a very expensive yacht.'

They all laughed, except Jonathan, and resumed the conversation that had foundered momentarily. Iris, angrily moving herself to what she hoped was an out-of-the-way corner, watched them in amazement, unable to believe that none of them had so much as lifted a finger to help when disaster seemed imminent, nor uttered one word of dismay, blame or even surprise. Or had she imagined the danger?

When they had all gone below and the yacht had cleared the headlands and was slipping peacefully southwards over the violet, Ionian water she asked Jonathan. He had all the wretched bits of rope set exactly right and was sitting by the wheel occasionally trimming it with a bare brown foot.

'Did you nearly get shipwrecked just now, coming out?'

He looked surprised.

'Could have, if something had snagged, I suppose. Nasty moment, that sudden gust, but something you should expect in that sort of place.'

'Why didn't they help you?'

He grinned.

'They trusted me.'

'Why didn't they scream and shout like ordinary human beings?'

'Bad form, old girl.'

'You are joking?'

'Well, yes, I was then.' He paused for consideration. 'It doesn't help, screaming and shouting.'

'It's natural. When you're frightened.'

'Lots of people scream and shout on yachts when things go wrong. They tend to go wrong very suddenly when you don't expect it—like it did back there. And you have to put it right very quickly, and if you panic everyone leaps up and gets in the way and it all goes to pieces. So it's best, really, to play it cool.'

'It's inhuman.'

'Yes, you could say that, I suppose.'

'Biggles, Jane says.'

'Biggles?'

'Jane says you're like Biggles,' Iris said, wishing even as she spoke that she wasn't saying it.

'Christ,' Jonathan said, and flushed deeply.

Iris looked out to sea, feeling terrible. Why was she always doing it? It was obvious that Jane didn't mean it as a compliment. It wasn't a remark to repeat, but she had repeated it. She was blushing as hard as Jonathan.

'Better go and make us a cocoa then,' Jonathan said.

'Cocoa?'

'He drank cocoa.'

'Did he?' Did Jonathan mean it, for Heaven's sake? Iris got up, sat down again. 'Do you want cocoa?'

'I wouldn't mind a cup of tea.'

She went below gratefully and put the kettle on. The gin-drinkers were now all snoring on their bunks, Jessica was reading and Charles and Amy were playing chess. The evening sun poured in with its gorgeous Mediterranean generosity and the reflection of the water rippled over the deckhead in a never-ending pattern, soothing and eternal. Iris could never get used to the surprising domesticity of

12

life below decks, the ritual of tea-making so matter-of-fact even when storms were raging and waves were breaking over the cabin-top. Waiting for the kettle to boil she stood on the companionway and gazed out.

'Where are you going?' she asked.

'I thought Kioni.'

'They never said Kioni.'

'That's their bad luck. Will you take her a moment while I look at the chart?'

Iris froze. 'Must I?'

'Yes.'

She went up. 'What shall I steer for?'

'Ithaca. That lump ahead. The big one, not the little one. Miss the little one.'

She stood trembling, watching the hazy blue hummock of Ithaca slumbering across the horizon, washed in golden-red sunlight, indistinct, a legendary island that she was half-convinced would disappear before Jonathan returned. It had to stay in place on the bows, not swing disastrously to port or starboard or even astern as was apt to happen when she took the helm. Why could she not be as the Merediths, dispassionate, wholly competent, calm? Inhuman.

But Jonathan wasn't inhuman.

He came back with the cups of tea before she had had much of a chance to run amok and took the helm again, and pulled a jersey on as the evening breeze ruffled the darkening surface of the sea. Martha heeled a little and raced silently for Ithaca. The golden sun was sinking abeam and the yacht was speared by the ruler of glittering light, the shadows of her mast and sails laid almost to the opposite horizon. The shores of Ithaca darkened and sharpened. Jonathan, standing at the wheel, was completely happy. Iris recognized the state and wondered at it, the situation to her so fraught with dire responsibilities, making a landfall safely on these now hostile steeply-rising shores. Iris hated above all things to be in charge of

13

important happenings, or even involved with them. Would she ever learn not to panic, to be cool and strong like Mrs Meredith? Mrs Meredith would stand firm in the path of charging elephants, Iris felt sure, or investigate a burglarish noise with a poker at the ready (although she was reported to have gone to pieces when Jonathan was kidnapped). Iris buried her nose in the tea-mug, wishing they were safe in harbour.

'Where is Kioni?'

'Round that far headland. Not the first one, the next.'

When they closed the headland Iris went below on a pretence, not wanting to be asked to do anything. Mr Meredith, rolling out of his bunk, said, 'Where are we, m'dear? Anywhere near a restaurant yet? I'm feeling peckish.'

'Yes, quite, I think.'

He glanced at his watch, looked surprised. Then he went up on deck. Murmurs of conversation, laughter. He came back, reaching for his pullover.

'The young devil! Hey, you lot, supper in fifteen minutes!'

And then it was merely a matter of finding something decent to go ashore in, while everyone else went about getting the sails down and the yacht bows-on the quay, the kedge laid out astern, decks cleared and tidy. When Iris went on deck the ominous landfall had turned into a snug berth in a land-locked harbour, a shore decked with welcoming lights and hillsides of dusking olive trees, music drifting out across the water. They went to a taverna and ate outside under a canopy of vines and Iris drank a lot of retsina to give herself more courage because she was so hopeless and because she was frightened of what she was doing and she needed the courage to go on with it. And with the retsina confusing her senses, reasons were forgotten and when the dinner was over she only wanted Jonathan again for all the old stupid reasons, the ones she could not help, because she loved him.

14

'Do you want to go for a walk before we go back?' she said to him as they left the restaurant.

'I don't mind. I wouldn't mind climbing that headland we came in round.'

Love did not appear to be in his mind at all, only mountaineering.

They climbed up the steep village street, crowded with children playing and men and women sitting on their doorsteps talking, and left the road where a track left it making westward through groves of pine and olive. Jonathan led the way, still climbing, and came out on to a brow from where there was a view down a valley that ran into the sea between two arms of rocks. He stopped, looking at it. There was the white thread of the road below and beyond it the deep violet-purple sea stretching away back the way they had come to Levkas, scarcely perceptible in the gathering dark, a darker smudge on the horizon. No sign of life anywhere; from below, faintly, the sound of waves breaking on an invisible shore and nearer at hand a soft breeze blowing in the pine tops, the scent of resin and spicy shrubs. Jonathan stood with his hands in his pockets; Iris sat down, wrapping her arms round her knees.

'Ulysses sailed from here,' Jonathan said. 'Not this cove but a bit farther round, opposite Cephalonia. I'd like to see it.'

'Not tonight?'

'No, it's too far. From the boat would be best. We could land, perhaps.'

He sat down beside her. 'It's amazing, everything that's happened round here in the past—the Greek legends, Roman galleys, the Turks, Byron liking the swimming, just like me, living here.'

'It's happened everywhere. Everywhere has a history.'

'Yes, that's true. Not everywhere had a Homer to write it up though. Ithaca's a bit special.'

'Did you do Greek?'

15

'I did a year of it.'

He seemed perfectly relaxed, not nervous of her at all. A silence fell between them, and he made no move to break it, to get up and go, but just sat gazing out to sea.

'Jonathan.'

She put her hand out to take his. This is where he would have jumped up as if stung by a bee if he had been truly frightened by her, but he just went on sitting there.

'What is it?'

'You know what it is.'

He turned and looked at her in quite cheerful surprise. 'Again?'

Hot flushes of embarrassment engulfed her. The retsina haze had been dispersed fatally by the hard climb up the mountainside and her confidence with it. She hung her head.

'I'm sorry.'

'*Iris!*'

He lay down, propping himself on one elbow and pulled her down against him.

'What do you mean, sorry? You are an idiot!'

'I know.'

'*No!* For heaven's sake—'

'What is it?'

'You shouldn't excuse yourself. I am more at fault than you, I'm such a bloody slow lover. I feel—oh, for God's sake, it's not for talking about—Iris ... oh, Iris!'

He sounded as tangled up as herself, and put his arm round her and lifted her face roughly up from where she had buried it in the front of his clean shirt, trying not to cry. The crying was mostly for hopeless love but he was not to know that; he must have known by now that she cried with incredible ease, for joy as much as sorrow. He started to kiss her, gently at first, and she forgot about crying, forgot about everything in fact, startled into the act of love which she had brought upon herself, lying on her back under the indigo sky and the vault of stars that had

16

looked on Ulysses, no less, and his Penelope on the same slopes; Iris found herself thinking again what a wonderful country this was to make love in ... no wonder the Latins were said to be such good lovers, with their sunny southern slopes to lie on and all that wine to chase away their reticence ... she started to laugh and Jonathan flung away from her and lay with his face buried in the pine needles, his back turned, shoulders heaving ... was that how it should be, Iris wondered? And reached out for him again, afraid she had offended, never knowing if she did the right thing or not.

It was true that Jonathan was as tangled up about making love to Iris as she seemed to be about it herself. He had no desire to make love to her until she started on it herself, and then he kissed her so as not to offend and after that things ran their course in what he thought of as a bit of a frenzy of which, in retrospect, he was not proud. Each time he vowed he would avoid another time like the plague, but somehow he never did. The act satisfied his body but did not leave him feeling anything but guilty and confused. Whether Iris enjoyed it or not he had no way of knowing. Sometimes she laughed and sometimes she cried. He could not really blame her, for he might well have done the same. Underlying his dissatisfaction was the great panic that there must be something wrong with him, that he could not take it in the light-hearted, boastful, funny way that his randier companions in the Prefects room at school appeared to do. The way they talked, the whole thing was absolutely great, but fantastic, man, and doubting never came into it. As long as you successfully laid the bird, conquest was all. Sex was for fun, not for mulling over. Jonathan supposed that with some girls he might feel the same, if the girl thought it was a lark too, a thing one learned together through trial and error, but Iris was not like that. Or, best of all, if one really loved the girl, then

17

there must be another dimension he could only guess at. And Jonathan found himself dreaming sometimes of the girl he wished Iris was: a quiet, serious girl of few words, who understood him without his having to say anything, who accepted, was sympathetic, and funny, who liked to climb mountains and ride. He didn't know of a girl in all his considerable acquaintance who fitted this bill although it did not seem very demanding. He wasn't asking for fabulous legs and big tits and hair like spun gold as well. In fact he rather thought of her as mousey and under-endowed, as far as physical appearance came into it. His mother tended to throw girls at him, summon him to awful lunch parties and tennis Sundays and introduce him to very pretty, terribly well-educated, self-confident girls who either frightened hell out of him or bored him rigid, or both. They had those sort at school, whom he managed to ignore pretty successfully, except when as Head Prefect he was forced to instruct, reprimand or otherwise communicate with. He would have ignored Iris if he could, but she was in a category of her own altogether.

The complications of another term at Meddington with Iris, which was his lot, to take Oxford entrance, loomed more seriously as the holidays drew towards their end. It was all right, this relationship in the wilds of Greece, but no way did he intend it to continue under the scrutiny of their fellow students at school.

'You do know that, don't you?' he asked her anxiously, when they were sitting together in the plane going home, some several thousand feet above French soil.

'I guessed,' she said simply.

'And don't tell anyone about it either.' It was callous, but he had to say it.

'You're ashamed?'

'No. But it's a private thing. I don't want to talk about it to anybody. Do you?'

'There isn't anybody, no.'

He felt brutally unkind, so much so that when he got

home he made an excuse to go off on his motor-bike and do a bit of climbing in the Lake District until it was time to go back to school. His friend Maurice Pumfrey declined to come because he had a conscience about work, being that sort of a character, but when they met again at school he said, for all he had accomplished, he might as well have had the time off with Jonathan. Jonathan had no conscience at all about work, in spite of the fact he was sitting Oxford entrance in November, the only reason he was back at Meddington.

'Haven't you done a stroke then?' Maurice asked in awe, after hearing about Greece.

'A bit of reading, that's all.'

They both had satisfactory A-level results. Jonathan had expected success, Maurice was amazed. Maurice was an introverted, shy, precocious boy who had no confidence in himself and did not make friends easily. He had a study next to Jonathan, having come new into the Sixth form.

'Did Iris go on the Greek trip too?'

'Yes.'

Jonathan was tempted to tell Maurice about what had happened between him and Iris, but decided not to. Having been so hard on Iris about keeping it confidential, it seemed unfair to talk about it himself, even to someone as discreet as Maurice. Besides, once back at Meddington, the whole Greek interlude became dreamlike in Jonathan's mind, the parochial, claustrophobic boarding school wrapping him in its familiar austere cotton-wool, divorced as it was completely from real life. It was miles from anywhere, in a beautiful wooded park with a wall round it. Spawning ground for hermits, Jonathan thought, for misfits, for nut-cases. He disapproved violently of the educational system his parents had chosen for him, but had not won his fight for freedom, and now had only a couple of months to go. He kept himself apart, had always done so, and had been made Head Prefect for his pains in order to coerce him into the system. He had conformed to his own disgust.

'And I'm afraid you'll have to carry on your duties for a month or so, as French has glandular fever," Fletcher, his house-master, informed him when he got back. French had been chosen as his successor. 'No sweat for you, as you've been so successful.' Fletcher smiled slyly. 'It worked, didn't it?'

Jonathan did not answer. He did not dislike Fletcher, who understood him very well.

'Get into Oxford and you will leave here in a blaze of glory, to your eternal consternation.'

Jonathan sighed. He was not at all sure he wanted to go to Oxford. His parents wanted it.

Iris, miraculously, kept out of his hair. He scarcely saw her at all. Her busy mother was doing a world tour and would be away until next spring; Jonathan's mother had already assumed Iris would come home with Jonathan at Christmas. Jonathan did not intend to take up the Greek relationship again. It was dishonest and he had never wanted Iris for a girl-friend.

A fortnight before Jonathan was to sit his first Oxford paper a girl called Jane whom he disliked intensely came to his study after supper.

'Can I have a word with you?'

'Yes.'

'It's private,' she said, glancing at Maurice who was looking in Jonathan's bookshelf for a German dictionary.

'He's a prefect,' Jonathan said, annoyed. If it was private in a personal sense the last thing he wanted was to be alone with Jane.

'Don't say I didn't warn you,' Jane said.

She came in and shut the door, and leaned against it.

'Look, Meredith, this is going to give you a shock.'

She was looking unlike her usual sharp-edged self, but positively sympathetic. The way she spoke gave Jonathan a nasty twinge of apprehension, more than the actual words. Jane was not a girl for confidences.

'You might not want Maurice to hear.'

'Oh, for heaven's sake, why not? He's a big boy now.'

'It's about Iris.'

'What about Iris?'

'Iris is—well, look, nobody knows, but I think ... She keeps being sick, you see, in the morning, and she thinks—and I think too—that she's pregnant.'

Whatever it was that Jonathan was expecting, it certainly was not this feminine confidence with its staggering implications.

'I'm the only one who knows and I can't keep it a secret much longer. She's got to get it sorted out. I came to you because—' Jane paused, kindly.

Jonathan knew perfectly well that it was not because he was the Head Prefect. He was outraged, horrified and furious. If it had been Iris herself standing in front of him instead of Jane he would have been hard put to it to have stopped himself from throttling her.

'I'm sorry,' Jane said, quite genuinely, seeing his state, 'I told you it was going to be a shock.'

'She told you—?'

'She told me it was yours, yes. She told me she wanted it, she did it on purpose, told you she was on the pill, made you do it, she said. She is a bit of a nut-case, really. I don't know what on earth to do so I thought I'd better pass it on to you. I mean, it's starting to show. It's three months.'

'She *wants*—?'

'Oh yes. It was all very much designed.'

'Jeez! It's no mistake? She's out of her mind!'

'Well, yes, I agree with you there.'

'She *can't*—'

'She can, you know.'

'I'm not playing at fathers! She doesn't expect that?'

'No, I don't think she does.'

'It makes me feel a swine, saying that. But no way—no way—oh, Christ!'

It was hard to accept. Jane sat on the table and Maurice

surfaced from the bookshelves, almost as pale with shock as Jonathan. He put the kettle on, like a First Aid man.

'The thing is, Jonathan, somebody's got to be told,' Jane said. 'Matron knows she's being sick and hasn't cottoned yet, but she must be suspicious, I would have thought. And Iris ought to go home. I've only passed it on to you because somebody's got to sort her out.'

The thought of Iris going home to his place and his parents finding out what had happened made Jonathan feel worse than the actual news that she was pregnant. Maurice hastily poured the boiling water over a teabag and made hot, sweet tea.

'It's for shock, man.'

'Her mother's away till half-way through next year.'

'It's all her fault really,' Jane said, 'when you think about it. Her mother, I mean.'

Iris wanted something, someone, to love, and had made herself a baby, Jonathan thought. He felt deeply, angrily, guilty for the way he had treated her, but knew he could not change it if it were to happen all over again. Nobody was ever going to believe the truth of it, that it was Iris herself who had been the seducer, not him.

'Do you want to talk to her?' Jane asked.

'No, I don't.'

'What do you want me to do?'

'You can do what you like.'

'You mean that?'

Jonathan hesitated. 'It's not my—' He stopped. He was going to say 'pigeon', but it seemed suddenly very inappropriate. If not his pigeon, it was his baby, whether he liked it or not. He felt more like bursting into tears, banging his head against the wall and saying. 'It's not fair!' like a three-year-old. He groaned, angrily.

'She'll have to tell Matron then. She needn't drag me into it, need she? Not now. I won't get out of it, not when my parents find out, but at least she doesn't want me to do an expectant father act already?'

22

It was strange how deeply he loathed Iris for what she had done. He did feel terribly like crying, but couldn't in company, fortunately. And not for Iris either, but purely for the injustice of what she had done to him.

'I told her I was going to tell you,' Jane said. 'So I've done it, and I'll tell her you said Matron ought to know and keep you out of it for now. Pretty brutal, but I can't say I blame you.'

Jane went to depart, opening the door, pausing. Jonathan knew that he ought to say something nicer, but couldn't.

'I'll tell you what happens,' she said.

When she had gone Jonathan sat on the hearth-rug in front of the gas fire and drank his cup of tea. Maurice sat with him in silent sympathy.

After about five minutes Jonathan picked up the German dictionary and flung it violently across the room at the wardrobe door and shouted, 'Jesus, what has she done to me?' And went out, slamming the door, and ran down the stairs and out into the rain.

Chapter 2

The only time Jonathan saw Iris during the next three days was from the platform in assembly, where he stood with the Head and Iris sat with the Upper Sixth in the choir. She certainly looked fatter, now that it had been pointed out to him; she also had a serene, self-satisfied expression which he had never seen before and which hardened him in his antipathy towards her.

On the third day, while the Head was blahing on about some boring arrangements for Christmas Jonathan noticed that two or three of the girls were looking at him in an amused sort of way. One of them said something to her neighbour, who looked at Iris, then back at him, and grinned widely. To his horror he felt himself flushing up. Then he decided he was being too sensitive, and they were only looking in the Head's direction because the Head was talking. But when at lunchtime he got his dinner and passed the sixth-form table he was acutely aware of a marked stoppage in the female chatter. And two seconds later, sitting down among his own kind, he was greeted with a studiedly offhand remark: 'There's some very strange rumours going round about you, Meredith. They do say as you've been getting young gels into trouble.'

He knew better than to rise to the bait and examined his steak and kidney pud critically.

'Young gels are nothing but trouble. I don't have anything to do with them.'

General scoffing greeted this remark.

'Who's that one you chased on horseback? The one on the race-course?'

'I was in front. She was chasing me.'

'They say you've been caught this time.'

'I've not heard about it."

'You will, mate. Matron's told Fletcher and Fletcher's going to tell the Head.'

'Where do you get all your information from, Bigmouth?" Jonathan was genuinely curious.

'The girls have told us. They've confided their troubles. One of them has got very big trouble indeed.'

'And what's this trouble got to do with me?'

'Half of it's yours.'

'Who says so?'

'The troubled one herself.'

'Wishful thinking,' Jonathan said shortly.

'She's an awful liar,' Murphy said cheerfully. 'Everyone knows that.'

'Yes, but she did spend a holiday in the heady Mediterranean with Meredith—that's true, isn't it, Meredith? And you know what all that topless sunbathing and the old vino leads to, don't you?'

'No. Tell me.'

It was difficult keeping his cool and even Murphy and some of the others who stuck up for him nevertheless were gazing at him somewhat meditatively—more so when Fletcher intercepted him as they left the dining-room and said, 'A word, Meredith. Come up with me.'

Jonathan walked with him down the long, stone-flagged corridor to the stairs, and his instinct told him things were serious. He had not until that moment much considered the school's feelings upon the predicament, only his own and his parents', and it now occurred to him that he had overlooked something equally unpleasant.

'The Head wants to see you. Before you go, I just want to know whether it's true or not—presumably you do know what the Head wants to talk to you about?'

'About Iris Webster?'

'Yes. The doctor saw her yesterday and confirmed that she's pregnant. She hasn't said anything officially about

25

who is responsible but rumour has it it's you.'

'Yes, it is. But—'

'No, save your defence for later. I only wanted to know that. You can tell the rest to the Head.'

Fletcher looked grieved and cool. They walked up the wide curving staircase together.

'He has sent for your parents, because they are Iris's next-of-kin, so to speak, while her mother is abroad. I think they are coming this afternoon—your mother is, at least. I don't know about your father.'

At the top of the stairs, outside the Headmaster's office, Fletcher stopped and turned to Jonathan.

'I want to warn you, Jonathan—I'm more sorry than I can say about this. Mainly I think, because you are going to get clobbered out of all proportion. The Head fought tooth and nail to prevent girls being admitted to Meddington but the governors overruled him. He isn't a worldly man, and problems of this nature are outside his sphere altogether. Iris is the one who will get away with it, because we all know that she is totally irresponsible and has had no sort of a chance with her home background, but you—well, you are the one who will have to bear the brunt of Armstrong's prejudices. You will find him totally unsympathetic and, I am afraid, not as balanced on this particular subject as he is on more academic matters. I just want you to be warned, that's all. You are the one, of all people, whom we did not expect to let us down.'

This little homily, and the prospect of his mother's imminent arrival, threw Jonathan into near panic as Fletcher left him outside the Headmaster's office. He had never been so frightened of an interview in his life and could not bring himself to knock on the door. However while he was fidgetting about outside it opened and the school secretary, Miss Allison, a fierce old bat who wore a tie and glasses on a chain, stood before him.

'Come in, Meredith. Mr Armstrong is waiting for you.'

She led him across her territory and to the inner door

26

which was open. Jonathan went in.

The Head, usually an urbane and quite affable man, sat and glared at him.

'Come here.'

Jonathan came.

'Is it true that you have fathered this child Iris Webster is expecting?'

Jonathan felt his insides quaking. The dark accusation, put in such Dickensian language, made him feel like a murderer rather than exactly the opposite.

'Yes, sir.'

He had a wild and unlikely vision of the possibility of Iris having seduced any number of gullible boys during her summer holidays: Greek waiters, the milkman, his cousin Charles ... but was not tempted to suggest it to Armstrong.

Armstrong glanced at his watch.

'Your mother should be here shortly. She knows the facts of Iris's pregnancy, nothing more. I suggest we wait and discuss the matter when she comes. There is no point in going over the same ground twice. I will only say to you, not in your mother's hearing, that I can forgive Iris for this disaster, for she has always been completely irresponsible, an unfortunate hysterical girl with a completely unsupportive home, but you—*you*, Meredith—were in a position of trust towards her and your behaviour is quite unforgivable. You have none of her excuses. I am quite confounded by your admission. Now, will you wait in the office with Miss Allison until your mother arrives.'

Jonathan retreated as requested, deeply disturbed by these attitudes of authority. He had never thought of himself as in a position of trust at all. News to him. And what was so special about his proving that his male parts worked, when at least half the sixth form had boasted of similar experiments as far back as the lower fifth? They had had lectures about the subject in school time and been taught how to do it, for Heaven's sake, with coloured slides and the substitution of long biological words for the short familiar ones they used among themselves. Trying to comfort himself with these arguments, he was compelled to sit and watch Miss Allison typing for forty minutes, trying to dull his nerves by wondering what she thought of sexual relations. Not a fruitful subject, he became steadily more despondent about what lay ahead. His mother was a formidable woman; 'motherly' was not an adjective that was applicable. And with the best will in the world, he could appreciate that the position he had put her in was very embarrassing. She was in charge of Iris for the time being, and would have to find her somewhere to go. But Iris had no relations and her mother was committed to concerts abroad and was unlikely to come home even for as dire a domestic hooha as this. She was where Iris had got her irresponsibility from. Or was it just that she loved her cello better than Iris? Not an unlikely possibility, to Jonathan's present way of thinking.

A bold knock at the door announced his mother.

She came in, looking as unlike a prospective grand-mother as Jonathan had feared, her nostrils dilated in the particular way he recognized as boding no good at all. He stood up, his mouth dry, and she gave him a surprised, tight-lipped appraisal.

'So?'

Had she been thinking, as she drove up from Raven-shall, that Iris's condition had been brought about by a Greek waiter, or the milkman, or her nephew Charles? In that moment Jonathan realized that she had been kidding herself that it had, and in that word, 'So?' she was for the first time admitting that the awful truth was as she had known in her heart of hearts all along. True to form, she made not the slightest formal gesture towards a greeting, to suggest that he was, when all was said and done, her dearest first-born son and heir. She removed her cold gaze to Miss Allison and said, 'Mr Armstrong is expecting me, I believe?'

'Yes, Mrs Meredith.'

Miss Allison went to the inner door, opened it and announced her arrival. Armstrong came out and they shook hands without any niceties being exchanged and Armstrong said immediately, 'I suggest we talk together in your son's presence, unless you have reasons for not doing so?'

'If he is responsible for what has happened, of course. There is absolutely nothing that should be kept from him.'

Which was putting it mildly, Jonathan thought in retrospect, the whole of the interview which followed being mainly grieved castigation of himself from a viewpoint so removed from his own that he could find no words with which to defend himself. He became so angry with their attitude that he retreated—as happened so often in front of his mother—into a tight shell of privacy; by keeping apart, he could keep control of himself. It seemed to him that neither of them could ever in all their lives have experienced normal human emotions of sympathy, love, doubt, sexual curiosity or even humour, so devoid did they seem to be of any understanding of how such a liaison as that between himself and Iris had come about. Such phrases as 'disgrace to the school' and 'complete ruin of her future' and 'impossible relationship' fell from their lips, having no relevance at all to what had truly happened; how could those ridiculous cliches have any bearing at all on those honey-smelling Grecian hillsides and soppy, sweet Iris drooping over his naked body with her crazy green-yellow hair smothering his face and her hands stroking him in that gorgeous way? The more they went on the more affectionate he felt towards her, the more divorced from his accusers. There was no way now he was going to describe how the relationship had started, to try and defend himself by describing Iris's advances, Iris's lies; outraged, he was above stooping to defend their behaviour.

'To get down to practicalities,' Armstrong said eventually, 'I will deal with Jonathan myself, but what do you think would be best for Iris? I can of course communicate with her mother, but her agent tells me there is no chance of her being able to return to this country.'

'I shall take Iris home with me. She is my responsibility for the time being. She can live at Ravenshall and have the baby there if necessary.'

Mrs Meredith had never been a woman for caring what the neighbours said, but Jonathan was astonished at this statement. Armstrong also looked surprised.

'I am told that she wants the baby,' she continued, 'Matron rang me, after I had spoken to you, and there is no question of an abortion. The background is Catholic, and Iris adamantly refused to speak of such a possibility, or so I was told. And as it seems the child is to be my grandchild, I would not wish it either. What happens after she has had it—well, we shall have had time to work something out. Jonathan meanwhile can take his Oxford entrance and find something to do away from home until he starts at university.'

'If it had not been so near the end of his time here, and the exams coming up, he would have been suspended,' Armstrong said. 'As it is, I will allow him to stay to take the entrance. But he will no longer hold prefect's office, nor be eligible for any of the Sixth form privileges. I will ask Mr Fletcher to make arrangements for him to move his study.'

'Yes, that is generous of you, Mr Armstrong. I do realize how deeply my son's behaviour has disappointed you, as it has my husband and I. I am really sorry that our pleasant relationship has to finish in this way.'

'Indeed. It comes the harder because Jonathan has until now been an outstanding pupil, a credit to Meddington.'

Listening to their goonlike conversation, Jonathan could scarcely believe what was happening to him. Deprived of a place in his own home, he was also to be deprived of his own place at school and the rank which, although something he had never particularly wanted, he now perversely had no wish to relinquish. The humiliation of being relegated to the ranks was pretty awful, not to sit on the top table for meals or use the prefects' common-room, to go back to a common dormitory and lose the privacy that he prized above everything else at school—petty as all these things in fact were, he could only see the sum total as dire punishment. He was banished from school life, as well as from home. He had been placed beyond the pale, like a leper.

He watched the leave-takings of his odious mentors through a haze of fury at the injustice meted out to him. Not one question had they asked him concerning his feelings, his view of the matter, his relationship with Iris. They had assumed he had acted out of lust and Iris out of a natural promiscuity.

When his mother had shaken hands with Armstrong and he had been dismissed, and the two of them were out on the landing at the top of the stairs, his mother turned to him and said bitterly, 'At least you might have used a contraceptive, you stupid boy! I would not say it in front of Armstrong, but I would have credited you with more intelligence on that score.'

And nothing would have dragged from him by now his puny excuse, his tale of Iris manipulating him, to get what she wanted, humiliation upon humiliation ... They went down the stairs together.

'I shall come back at the weekend to collect Iris, when she has packed all her things. We can discuss it more calmly then. Neither of us are in a fit state at present. You have behaved disgracefully and should be extremely grateful that Mr Armstrong has not suspended you.'

He went down the stairs with her in silence and saw her to the front door, opened it for her like the well-brought-up boy he was. She went out without another word, climbed into her car and roared off. Jonathan shut the door and stood with his forehead pressed against the glass panel, trying to fight down an overwhelming feeling of betrayal. The injustice they had meted out to him made him feel physically sick; he was breathing as if he had been running hard and had to restrain a strong impulse to smash his fist through the glass he was leaning against.

The school was quiet, calm in mid-lesson, familiar and cosy about him as a worn coat. He had never received any punishment in all his time there more severe than a ritual ticking-off, a detention or two, nothing to prepare him for this gunning-down in his last week or two before leaving. He went slowly back to his study, and stayed there alone until Fletcher came at four o'clock and told him to clear all his things out; there was a bed for him in Dormitory 6, and a locker and wardrobe out in the corridor.

'You might as well start now, get it cleared before tea.'

Prefects took tea in the Prefects' common-room. He was not allowed to go there, but no way was he going to go anywhere else. He would bloody starve first. He started blindly to fling things out of his wardrobe on to the bed.

'Hey, what's up?' It was Maurice, standing in the doorway. 'Aren't you coming down to tea?'

'No.'

'Where've you been all afternoon? What's wrong?'

'I've been demoted. Got to move out.'

'Where to, for God's sake?'

'A bloody dormitory.'

'What?' Maurice couldn't believe it. 'But it was a private thing, in the holidays—you and Iris . . . and why you, when it was her fault? It's crazy, demoting you. It's got nothing to do with it.'

Jonathan could not bring himself to explain. He could not take what had happened, he decided. The indignation kept welling up; the unfairness of it was unacceptable.

'I'm going to push off,' he said to Maurice. 'I've got my motor-bike. I'll find somewhere I can cool off, think what's best.'

His motor-bike leathers were in the wardrobe, along

with his crash helmet. He started to push them into a zip case, along with his spare-time clothes, jeans and an anorak. Maurice watched miserably, not trying to stop him.

'You could sleep in my room tonight—no one'd find out,' he suggested.

'It won't be any better, even if I do. And Fletcher will check up on me tonight, I know it. I've got some cash, and a cheque-book, enough to see me through for a few days.'

'Where will you go?'

'I don't know yet. Anywhere'll do, away from here.'

The thought of taking the bike out on a fast road somewhere was suddenly irresistible. It did a ton, and doing a ton never failed to make him feel fantastic. He needed it badly.

'Will you do me a favour and take this bag out to the bike shed? If anyone sees me with it they'll guess what I'm up to. But if it's already there, I can slip out when everyone's at supper and with luck I won't be seen.'

'They'll know you're missing, come bedtime.'

'If Fletcher asks, tell him I've gone for a walk, to think about things. Put him off if you can. I doubt if they'll set up a search-party—it suits them if I clear off, after all, having "disgraced the school" as they put it. I'm a big boy now, I've got the vote. I can do what I bloody well please by law.'

'You can go home to my place if you like. My parents would put you up. I'll give them a ring.'

'No, thanks all the same.'

'Jeez, I wish you weren't going.'

'Well—' Jonathan shrugged. His plan for action had made him feel a hundred per cent better already. There was no way he could face going into the dining-hall and not taking his place at the top table, and going into assembly in the morning, not on the platform but in with the rabble below the Prefects' benches. That was public humiliation, which he could not face. If it had been deserved, he might have come to terms with it, but his

33

pride rebelled.

'What about your Oxford entrance? Are you coming back?'

'I don't know.'

He wasn't a rebel by nature, after all. A fast fling on his lovely BMW, a few days off and getting drunk somewhere, and he might see it all in a different light—enough, at least, to turn up for the exams upon which, one assumed, his future depended. Or so they said. He had never seen his future with any clarity at all and had no great faith in the advantages of a degree. His father had never got a degree and he had made a pile. Mr McNair the horse-dealer drove a great Merc as well as a six-horse Bedford and enjoyed life no end and he hadn't got a degree either. Talking of McNair. . . .

'There's someone I could go to, stay a day or two.' He had gone to the McNairs after another crisis at Meddington and got cured. Peter, his contemporary, was now working at a National Hunt stable in Berkshire somewhere, and lived in a caravan. He could sleep on Peter's floor. Peter (after laughing his head off) might come up with some sound advice. Peter saw things clearly. Jonathan felt he could see nothing clearly at all any more.

'I had an address—a letter somewhere.' He hunted around in his desk drawer and found Peter's scrawl. (Peter hadn't got a degree either, and only two O-levels, after skiving off school several weeks a term) 'I'll go there—it's a friend.'

Maurice looked worried, opened his mouth to protest, but at that moment Fletcher came in.

'Come on, Meredith, get a move on. I want you out and the place tidy by five.'

'I'm packing, sir.'

He zipped his escape case up so that Fletcher would not see what was in it.

'I'd like to talk to you about this business, when you've finished here. Come to my room.'

'Yes, sir.'

Blast it, Jonathan thought. Fletcher departed, and Jonathan said, 'There's no point my hanging about, in that case. I can't stand any more jawing. I'll push off now.'

'I'll come down with you.'

Having made the decision about five minutes previously, Jonathan could not wait to put it into practice. The furious emotions of the afternoon had been channelled into constructive adventure. Even if he changed his mind come midnight, it would air his overwrought brain, give him a breather, and if he got into trouble for it there was nothing else they could do to him now.

'I'll leave my room. Someone else can pack it up, as if I've died. "Go through my effects" as they say. There's a few odds and ends, private like—can you take them?'

'Yeah.'

Jonathan gathered them together, the sort of things that might go missing—his camera, a pair of binoculars, a few books and tapes—and Maurice put them in his locker next door. He picked up the bag.

'I'll carry it for you, in case anyone is curious.'

Most people were at tea but there was no way they could get down to the bike-shed without being seen. They went purposefully, as if on an errand, out of the front door and across the gravelled drive to the garage complex opposite, and safely round the back to the bike shed without anyone accosting them.

'If anyone asks—and they will—tell 'em I told you I was just going out for a run, to think things over. They'll probably take that okay, and not ring home to say I've run off or anything dire.'

Jonathan had unzipped the bag and was pulling his bike gear on. It was a sharp, grey day, the end of October, with a hint of drizzle in the air. There were already some lights on in the school building, distant shouting from the junior football pitch; a thrush singing loudly from the cedar tree, a typical Meddington dusk with no hint to suggest that this

35

day was different from any other and quite possibly his last sight of these familiar surroundings. Jonathan did not know what he intended to do at that moment. Maurice passed him the crash helmet.

'God, I hope it's going to start.'

Even if he was now unrecognizable inside his gear, everybody knew the bike, and the only way out was across the front of the school, no way to be effected quietly.

'Look, don't get into trouble on my behalf.'

Maurice had secured the bag on the back seat. 'No, don't worry. If you don't come back, write me and say what you're up to.'

'Okay. Thanks for everything, Maurice.'

Maurice grinned. 'Good luck.'

The bike fired with a blast that sent the rooks up out of the cedar tree. Jonathan hoped that his raucous exit would not be taken as defiance; it was as unobtrusive as he could make it, which wasn't saying much.

Maurice's desolate figure raised a hand in farewell.

Jonathan opened the throttle and roared off down the drive.

Chapter 3

At nine-thirty on a dismal autumn night the whereabouts of Peter McNair, Markpen House and the thirty-three race-horses resident there were hard to trace. Having done ninety-eight, a hundred and seven, and a hundred and fifteen on three respective bits of motorway, dined on fish and chips in Reading and drunk too much in Swindon, Jonathan found himself half an hour later bogged down in a muddy lane miles from nowhere with nothing in his headlamps but windswept thorn trees and tractor ruts two feet deep. An ex-jockey in Swindon had given him directions. They could have been right, Jonathan supposed. He was cold and tired and the day's events had become muddled in his mind and nothing like so important as finding Peter and somewhere to lay his buzzing head.

He examined what he could see, which wasn't much, and divined a lot of hoof-prints overlaying the tractor patterns which was encouraging. He pressed on, wheels spinning, and came out on to a hard road crossing at right-angles and a board which pointed to right and left, with 'Markpen' inscribed on the rightward arm. Lights glimmered hopefully some five hundred yards farther on. There was a drive which led into a farmyard and a house with a light over the porch. A horse whinnied in the sudden stillness as Jonathan turned off his engine.

He sat a moment, gathering his wits, then got off and knocked at the door.

'Peter? You a friend of his then?'

The man who came to the door looked not unlike Peter, an older and tireder version.

'Yes.'

'He's got a caravan up the back. Go through the yard, and the second yard where the horses are. You'll see the caravan.'

'Thanks.'

Jonathan followed directions and found the caravan in his headlights, parked beside a haybarn. Light shone through tatty curtains. Jonathan parked his bike in the shelter of the big barn and knocked for the second time.

'Come in!'

Peter was lying on his bed in fuggy squalor, reading 'Sporting Life', a transistor blasting pop. He looked up amiably.

'Introduce yourself.'

Jonathan lifted off his helmet and unwound a few revolutions of scarf, and Peter leapt off the bed, his face lighting up.

'God, Meredith! What are you doing here? Had another brainstorm? Come for sanctuary? Hey, come in, man. Shut the door. What's that nice school of yours doing, letting you go free on a working night?'

Jonathan grinned. 'They don't know. Sanctuary it is. You're a useful guy for running to.'

'A wonder you found me. It's real back-of-beyond here, if you haven't got any transport. Well, I've got transport, but as it only does ten miles to the gallon I can't say I use it much.'

'Christ! You got a Rolls?'

'No, it's an Oldsmobile hearse, nineteen fifties vintage. Belongs to a friend of mine—in hospital at the moment—came off at Kempton and stove his head in a bit, told me to look after it like it was my own. Well, I keep the bird-shit off it and start the engine every now and then, but my skinflint brother doesn't pay me enough to keep it in gas.'

'That your brother then?'

'You saw him? Yes. This is his place. It's a dump. I'd push off if I had half a chance. He's got a head lad runs the

38

place—we don't see eye to eye, to put it mildly. My brother's got problems—wife, kids, all on the rampage—bad back, the virus—you name it, he's got it—I'd like to go to a decent place. But what's your story? You're not in trouble are you?'

'Well—'

Jonathan took off a few outer layers and Peter cleared a place for him close to the Calor gas heater, and made large mugs of hot coffee. Thawing out, Jonathan told him how Iris had landed him into trouble. Peter knew Iris, his home base being close to Jonathan's. They had been friends, through horses, for several years, and their parents were friends too. Peter had brushed with Mrs Meredith himself on several occasions and knew the score. Jonathan did not have to describe her displeasure; Peter knew the lady's temperament only too well.

'These women, they all stick together these days. Instead of her getting tossed to the lions for naughty behaviour, it's you. They call it women's lib.'

'It's her having done it on purpose that gets me. If it had been a genuine slip-up I could have taken it. But saying she was on the pill—lying to me, after all I've done for her!' His genuine, childish self-pity almost choked him again. He really had suffered that girl, invited her home out of pity, even saved her wretched life when she had flung herself in the river in one of her tantrums, endured any amount of teasing at school because of her histrionic devotion.

'She must have been a bit desperate—to have a kid, I mean. When you think, it's quite a step.'

'She was going to college to study music. She didn't want to go. I think it was a way out for her.'

'Some way out!'

'Jane—this girl at school—said she really wants a baby.'

Peter grinned. 'And you?'

'Bloody hell! I don't want to think about it. I'm not going home while she's there, I can tell you. Look at the

39

position it puts me in. Imagine friends calling "Who's this then?" And my mother doing a grandmother act ... I mean, I'd have to marry the girl, wouldn't I?'

Peter considered. 'It's very odd, yes. Odd of your mother mostly, chucking you out and taking the girl instead, as if it was your fault entirely.'

'They all think it is. They say it's to be expected of Iris, her being a nutcase anyway, but not for me.'

'The Head Prefect?'

'Well, yes. That's what they mean.'

Jonathan could let go with Peter, and felt better for expressing his baser thoughts about the whole business. Peter already knew the worst, the most unworthy twists of his character, knew him at rock-bottom; one did not have to pretend, or even keep silent. It helped to rabbit on, to curse and rave.

Peter said, 'It's your bloody upbringing—rarified—all this upper-class twittery ... not how we carry on at the Comprehensive, you know. Abortion for her, a belting for you and back to square one, same as if nothing's happened. Stands to sense you're all nutters, shut up in a place like that. Have you run away just for a night, by the way, or for good?'

'Haven't decided yet.'

'You stay. It's really good to see you. I'm bloody fed up as well. This job's hopeless.'

'Why? This is a good yard, isn't it?'

'It's successful, yes. But my position's—well ... because I'm the guv'nor's brother, the head lad—Eddie Wenlock he's called—he keeps me in my place. He's frightened if I'm any good I'll get his job—which is virtually head trainer, my brother being so crocked up. He's good at the job but he's hard as nails and he really hates me. Poor old Geoff—my brother, that is—he can see what's happening but he can't afford to lose Eddie. I can appreciate that—I mean, I don't want the job, that's what's so bloody stupid. I'm after being a jockey, not a trainer. Anyway, to put it simply, we hate each other's guts, and as he's the boss it's me who suffers.'

'Jeez, your father was bad enough. I thought leaving him was going to be roses all the way.'

'Yeah, so did I.'

It helped, in a strange way, Peter being down the drain as well, to have a fellow in adversity.

'You stay for a bit, you'll see. We're always a lad or two short so you can earn your keep, ride out as well. Being a friend of mine, you'll probably get the same treatment.' Peter laughed.

'A couple of days, perhaps. I've got to work something out.'

But Jonathan was too tired to think any more. Peter gave him some spare cushions on the floor and a sleeping bag and he was out as soon as his head touched down.

It was still dark when Peter's alarm went off. If Jonathan had spent a week deciding how best to take his mind off his insoluble troubles, he could not have done better, he quickly realized, than pitch himself into Peter's routine.

Peter fell over him, groping for the lamp, apologized, offered his still-warm bed.

'Lie in for a bit. Until we ride out—give you another hour. You can have my spare jods. I'll leave them out for you. I'll fix a horse for you.'

Peter threw on some clothes and went out. Jonathan, still in his sleeping bag, humped himself into Peter's bed, slept another five minutes, then lay listening to the general stirring of the yard outside, motor-bikes arriving, shouts and laughter, a horse whinneying. It was freezing cold in the caravan. Jonathan compared his situation with how it would be if he were still at Meddington, and knew he was considering the day with more optimism here than he would be in his common dorm in the equally cold Meddington. He got out and started to dress.

41

He was familiar with racing routine, nervous more of Eddie Wenlock than riding a racehorse. He surmised that any friend of Peter's was likely to get the same treatment as Peter at the gentleman's hands, and was proved right as soon as he introduced himself.

'Yeah, well, if McNair thinks he's having you on one of his so he can get out of riding out twice, he can think again. You can ride one of Jim's pair—give him a break. He reckons he's got a dose of flu just starting. You can ride, I take it?'

'I've ridden in quite a few point-to-points.'

'We'll soon see. That's Jim over there. Go and see him.'

Graciousness was not Eddie Wenlock's forte, Jonathan decided. A stocky, middle-aged man, he had a belligerent chin and a manner to match, and was not much gentler with the horses than he was the lads. There were about ten lads, a mixed bunch of all ages arrived from the nearest village, hunched down into muddy anoraks; Jim was a spotty youth touchingly grateful for Jonathan's offer to take his horse.

'That's great. It pulls like a train and I feel like I'm made of cotton-wool this last day or two. He'll try and bolt when you canter but if you're ready for him you'll be okay. I always stay at the back.'

Jim fetched Jonathan his crash-helmet and Jonathan led out the seventeen-hand grey beast that was now his responsibility. It quivered with well-being, sniffing the raw downland air into the great black pits of its distended nostrils. Looking at it, Jonathan wondered doubtfully how one was expected to stop a horse of such obvious power bolting if it really felt like it. He might find out later.

It was barely light as the string moved out down the drive. A steel grey dawn over the darker humps of the downs gave no hint of sun; the only brightness was in the sprinkle of lights gleaming from the village that nestled far below the ridge they followed. The string of horses padded over the soaking turf, the riders jostling knees, gossiping, some smoking. It was bitterly cold. Jonathan looked for Peter and they rode together briefly—until the trainer caught them up on his hack and dispatched Peter with some sharp comments.

'Get up to the front where you belong. You want all your attention on that bloody horse, or we'll have more trouble with it before we're through.'

Peter departed. His horse, a chunky powerful-looking dark bay, put its ears back at Eddie's disagreeable voice, as if echoing Peter's own opinion, and strode on with an impressive, ground-devouring action.

Another lad moving up to take his place, Jonathan asked him what Peter was riding.

'That's Dogwood. He's our National hope.'

'Looks the sort.'

'Yeah, he's a hell of a horse. All ways round. No one else'll ride him save Peter.'

'Why not?'

'Got a mind of his own. If he says no, you've had it.'

'Peter's got a way with that sort of horse,' Jonathan said, remembering their Pony Club days. Peter only liked difficult horses. He said it was boring if they always did what was expected.

'Yes, it's a fact,' the lad said. 'Eddie would have got rid of Dogwood by now if he'd had his way. Says it needs a bullet.'

Several of Peter's animals in the past had needed a bullet. The phrase made Jonathan smile. Humans ran true to form just like horses. By running away, was he, too, acting in character? He would just about be getting up now, if he'd been at school. But better the grey character beneath him and the bantering lads than the company he would be sharing at school today. He was a status snob. It was a form of vanity, he supposed, not a sin he had ever felt before that he was guilty of.

He survived the ride, and was thinking about breakfast by the time they came back to the stableyard, dropping down off a steep shoulder of close-cropped turf to a gate close by Peter's caravan. Peter waited for him by the gate, pulling out of his place at the front of the string. When Jonathan came up to him he nudged Dogwood to go alongside, but the horse stopped in the gateway. Jonathan rode on to give him a lead, but Dogwood still refused to move. Jonathan pulled up and turned round, and saw Eddie coming up behind Peter on his hack.

'Do you never bloody listen to instructions, McNair?' Eddie bawled. 'Get that horse going!'

'If you go ahead of me, I'll get him going,' Peter said evenly.

Eddie carried a long schooling whip in his hand. He rode his hack sharply towards Dogwood and gave the horse two blistering cuts across the hocks which Peter was quite unprepared for, and never even saw. Dogwood dropped his head and gave two almighty bucks and Peter shot out of the saddle and landed with some force against an iron water tank that collected the rain off the barn roof. Dogwood still the wrong side of the gate, started to graze as if nothing had happened.

Jonathan slipped off his horse and went across to Peter, startled by Eddie's stupidity. Peter looked equally startled, not quite sure what had happened. He had hit his nose on the tank and it was bleeding copiously and he was covered in the wet mud the horses had churned up, having landed full-length in the worst of it.

Jonathan fished out a handkerchief and handed it to him.

Eddie had caught Dogwood's reins but the horse still would not come through the gate.

'You!' he bawled at Jonathan, 'Put your horse away and fetch me a lungeing-rein from the tack-room. And a whip. Hurry up! I don't want to spend all day out here.'

'You okay?' Jonathan said doubtfully to Peter.

'All in a day's work with our Eddie,' Peter muttered.

'Move!' Eddie bawled.

Jonathan took his horse back to Jim and enquired about the lungeing-rein. One of the older lads fetched one out, and a whip, and handed them over, not saying anything. Jonathan noticed that they were all acutely interested in what was happening, the usual idle chatter having come to a halt. He went back and handed over the gear. Eddie had dismounted, and ordered him to take the hack, throwing him the reins.

'Come here, you,' he snapped at Peter.

Peter squelched across, holding the handkerchief to his face.

'Get back on. I'm going to teach this horse a lesson. You let him get away with murder and it's time he learned who's boss.'

'He's not a three-year-old,' Peter said stubbornly. 'He's twelve. It's the way he is. You aren't going to change him now, not by beating him up.'

'I'll be the judge of that. Less of your lip. Get up there and do as you're told.'

Peter got back into the saddle while Eddie fastened the long lunge-rein to the horse's bit. Then he picked up the whip.

'We'll canter him until he's had enough, then we'll get him through that gateway, with or without the whip. Come on, buck your ideas up, lad.'

For good measure he unleashed the long whip in Dogwood's direction, letting out the rein at the same time. Peter stuffed his handkerchief away hastily to gather up the reins and was just in time to survive the first buck fired by the indignant Dogwood. Jonathan saw him jam his knees in and lean back. His spine was supple as a gymnast's.

Leaning thoughtfully over the fence to watch, Jonathan saw that Eddie was using Dogwood's behaviour as a splendid excuse to discomfort Peter, who was in an unenviable situation. The other lads, having put their horses away, also stood watching, the scene more compel-

45

ling even than breakfast which was apparently the next event on the agenda.

Dogwood could escape from neither the rein which held him nor the whip chasing his hind-quarters, and circled the trainer in a series of gigantic plunges. The ground was very slippery and as Dogwood went faster and faster he tore great strips of turf out of the ground with his skidding hooves and looked as if he would go down at any moment, very likely pinning Peter underneath him. Peter, riding with short racing stirrups, kept his precarious seat by pure balance, white with rage beneath the blood and mud which splattered his face. Eddie drove the horse on until he lapsed into a wild bucketting canter, and then whipped him towards the gate which he baulked at again, with a vicious duck of his head and shoulder which Peter this time sat with impressive skill. Round a second time and he reared, and was not far from going over backwards.

When he came down Peter, wiping his face with the back of his hand, said, 'Who are you trying to kill, me or the horse?'

'You'd neither of you be any loss,' Eddie said shortly.

Jonathan could see that he was now in a quandary, not getting his way and not being able to give way without losing face. Fortunately for him one of the lads called out to him, 'The guv'nor wants you to go to the house, Mr Wenlock, soon as you can.'

'That's bloody lucky for you, McNair,' he said to Peter. He went up to the trembling Dogwood and unclipped the lunge-rein. 'You stay in that saddle and get him through that gate before you go for your breakfast. Between those two gateposts and no others. Else you stay out there all day.'

He departed, the lads scattering out of their interested groups as he turned in their direction. Jonathan waited until he had disappeared and said to Peter:

'I see what you mean.'

'You got the impression he doesn't like me?' Peter

almost smiled.

'Roughly, yes. What are you going to do?'

'Calm this fellow down first. Then breakfast.'

Jonathan could not see how Peter was going to achieve the first step towards his breakfast: get through the gate, for Dogwood was obviously a horse of strong principle and looked as unlikely to change his mind about that particular issue as Peter did about respecting his trainer. But Peter walked the horse patiently around the field a few times, talking to him until he settled and then, on his next circuit, called to Jonathan as he passed, 'Shut the gate, will you?'

Curious, Jonathan did as he was told. Peter put Dogwood into a canter, circled calmly three times and then came down fast towards the gate and jumped it without any fuss. Pulling up, he said, 'Better open it again. No one will ever know.'

'Is that in the book of rules?' Jonathan enquired as Peter slid out of the saddle.

'My rules, yes. Not Eddie's, I daresay.' Peter opened the gate.

Jonathan put the hack away and joined Peter who was rubbing Dogwood down in his box. A marked expression of contempt was stamped in the horse's demeanour; he was not a spirit easily subdued, Jonathan guessed. His eyes were bold and challenging, although rimmed with warning white; his ears large and mobile. He had a big crooked star and a raffish forelock, an untidy upstanding mane in spite of Peter's ministrations, adding to the general impression of individuality. Standing about sixteen and a half hands, substantial and compact, he curiously had the look of a small horse, enormously thick through the girth and short in the back, and with scarred, veteran legs that lacked the fineness of pure blood. Seven-eights, Jonathan guessed, and all go. He was impressed by him, and did not think he deserved Eddie Wenlock's censure.

'The man's an idiot, you can see,' Peter agreed. 'He's

47

done his best to turn this horse into a rogue—nobody else wants to handle him now, thanks to Eddie's forcing methods. He doesn't respond to bullying, but that's the only way Eddie knows. They're talking about sending him to the sales, or even having him put down. Last time he went racing he wouldn't start, but that was only Eddie upsetting him in the paddock.'

'What does the owner say?'

'The owner's my brother, and he's got more pressing problems. Let's go and get some food.'

Peter rubbed his anorak down with a wisp of straw, merging the copious splashes of blood and mud into a uniform sludge, and paused briefly to wash his face under the yard tap. His nose was swollen and gashed over the bridge.

'That was no joke, the way Eddie treated you,' Jonathan said.

'No. I told you he enjoys doing me down.'

They joined the other lads in the tack-room which was big enough to be half kitchen, where a village woman was lobbing out tea and fried egg sandwiches. Peter got ribbed for his display, but with obvious sympathy. It was plain that the trainer was generally disliked. Jonathan could see that, although Peter shrugged it off, he was thoroughly disenchanted with his morning's work.

'If you're on the run, how about if I join you?' he suggested to Jonathan. 'We could set up something together.'

Jonathan was not sure if he was serious, but after they had ridden out again and fed the horses, and had two hours to themselves in the caravan until teatime, it transpired that he was. Peter lay on his bed, picking morosely at the flakes of paint on the caravan wall, squinting down his swollen nose.

'I've been thinking of leaving since I've seen how the land lies here, but I don't want to go back to Daddy, for heaven's sake, and jobs are few and far between. But if you've dropped out too, perhaps we could do something together.'

'Have I dropped out?' Jonathan wasn't sure.

'Well—what you said ... you can't go back if you're going to be treated like a third former. Even I can see that that's the real stopper.'

'Mmm.' Peter was right. Jonathan knew that he was postponing facing facts. 'And what is this something anyway?'

Peter did not reply at once. He sat gnawing his fingernails for some time, and then spoke hesitantly.

'That horse—Dogwood—he's on the black list too. But he's entered in the Grand National, and my brother's promised me the ride. Chances like that don't happen every day—you know that. But if we stay here much longer that horse won't run in any race again, let alone the National, because Eddie's breaking his spirit. So if I go, I take the horse with me.'

'Christ!' Jonathan had been thinking of the two of them on the motorbike, with a toothbrush apiece, looking for jobs somewhere. This put a new complexion on it. 'That's a bit of a liability, tagging along a nag.'

'Yeah, but with two of us—one could go on training him and one could get a job and earn the wherewithal. Real joint effort. You could do the training, if you like, and me the job.'

'You'd have to keep riding to be fit.'

'Well, we can work that one out. But two of us, Jonathan, it could be done. With only one, it's really very difficult. I've thought about it often enough. He's such a bloody good horse, you see, real National type. He jumps a house and he stays for ever. I mean, I don't have a hope in hell of winning, but getting round ... yes, that's everybody's dream, isn't it? I know my brother would go along with the idea. Getting rid of me and the horse would smooth things in this yard no end.'

'What would you do—ride away? Where to?'

'No, there's a trailer I can take, and the old hearse would tow it a treat. Where to—that's a toss-up. Somewhere we could train, a beach perhaps. And a job not too far away. Bit tricky. But I've saved up quite a bit of money, enough to live on for three or four weeks.'

'I've got a bit too.'

Jonathan thought about going back to school, and about what Peter was suggesting. He thought about his Oxford entrance, his responsibility to his parents, his future, his prospects. Once all that had carried quite a lot of weight with him: he was known as 'responsible'. They had used it as an accusation over the Iris thing. They had blamed and punished him for something that was not his fault. The way he felt at the moment they had foregone his loyalty. Why shouldn't he go with Peter and rough it? He had always hankered after a taste of 'real life', feeling that he had missed out in many ways through the cushioning of wealth and privilege. He had never been all that enthusiastic about going to Oxford. Given the Grand National as an alternative, he was sorely tempted.

'I've thought about it since the summer,' Peter said. 'If you're game, I'll see my brother about Dogwood. He'd have to be the official trainer, on paper, and keep him entered, do the paperwork—if all goes well, that is. I'm sure he'll agree. What do you think?'

It was hard to give up eighteen years of conditioning in a moment. But the opportunity appealed, out-of-joint as he was with his proscribed path.

'I'll tell you tomorrow. Sleep on it. I think so, at the moment.'

Even as he said it, he knew the answer was yes. It was only his renowned sense of responsibility that postponed the answer. As if he knew, Peter went up to the house to talk the idea over with his brother.

'It's obvious he can't wait to see the back of me,' he reported, somewhat bitterly. 'Even offered to fill the hearse up with petrol.'

'We have to go in a hearse?'

'I'll show it you. It's really comfortable in the back, and miles powerful enough to tow old Dogwood.'

The hearse, under wraps in one of the barns, looked like something out of a Hollywood movie, a flash, low-slung job with a lot of chrome-work, and on the roof a sort of silver fender with knobs at each corner and a glittering cross surmounting all.

'You can sleep where the stiffs used to go. Steve's got a mattress in it, look. It'll suit us fine. He put a tow-bar on it too. It's made for the job.'

'What about the motor-bike?'

'That can go in the trailer with Dogwood, in the other partition.'

There was no way Meddington could win after that.

Peter's brother asked them up for a meal in the evening, and it was plain that the idea was perfectly acceptable to him. 'Give me three months and I'll be fit enough again to take over in the yard. Just at the moment I can't afford to be without Eddie. In many ways he's a very able man and that's what I need. He's not likeable, but that comes second just at the moment. So you clear off for the winter and we'll start again next season, God willing. You'll have to give the old horse a race or two before Aintree. See how he goes and I'll make a few entries for you when the time comes, and I'll keep him in the big race unless you tell me otherwise.'

'We'll go tomorrow then, after riding out. You can tell Eddie.'

'Where will you go?'

In the end they tossed for it, North, South, East or West. It came out East.

'East coast then. Suffolk, say, or Norfolk.'

'You'll need your thermal underwear. Nothing between you and the Arctic out there.'

'Bracing,' Peter agreed. 'I'm going to get a warm job in a chip-shop or summat and Jonathan's doing the exercising.'

51

They both slept fitfully, excited by their prospects. Or lack of prospects, more accurately.

The next day they worked without incident until lunch-time and then prepared to move off. Jonathan had virtually no luggage anyway, and by the time the horse's gear was loaded—rugs, tack, stable tools and impedimenta, and a fair measure of feed, hay and straw—there was little room for anything else. They threw in sleeping-bags, the portable gas-lamp, a small camping cooker, a box of food, breadknife, tin-opener, matches.

'It's like going on holiday,' Peter remarked. He fished out his documents, his riding licence, his driving licence.

Looking doubtfully at the hearse, Jonathan asked, 'Got your Funeral Director's licence for this then?'

'I've got its log-book, good thing you mentioned it. If we ever get an address, I'll write Steve and tell him we're keeping it ticking over for him.'

They hitched on the two-horse trailer which Peter said was more or less his—'It's Dad's anyway'—and loaded Dogwood (who thought he was going racing and started crashing around with excitement) and the motor-bike which Dogwood, expecting equine company, found hard to understand. Jonathan kept trying to stifle an instinct that told him what they were doing was crazy. Once in the hearse with Peter, there would be no ratting back to Meddington ... wasn't already, in fact. He laughed, glad to be committed.

'This is no laughing matter,' Peter said, grinning, getting into the driving seat.

The fender job on the top of the hearse was doubling as roof-rack and two bales of hay and one of straw were snuggled comfortably fore and aft of the impressive cross. Peter reached over and opened the passenger door.

'Come on, Chief Mourner.'

Jonathan got in. Just as they drove out of the yard Eddie

came up in his Landrover and was forced to pull on one side for them. He stuck his head out of the window and bawled, 'Where are you off to?'

'The Crematorium,' Peter shouted back.

'Which way the crematorium,' Jonathan muttered, fishing out the motoring map Peter had stuffed in the glove-locker.

'Due East. This job's got every bit of gear save a compass.'

'Keep the sun on your right then. Stop when you get to the sea.'

'There's the little detail of London getting in the way.'

'Up a bit then.'

'We'll end up at home.'

'Up and *on*—too low down and it's all bloody mudflats. Suffolk'll do.'

A beeline was hard to come by, all the main roads crossing them as they radiated from London, but they navigated successfully towards the far-flung shores they had decided upon, at one point passing a mere twenty miles from their own homes.

'Pity I can't call for some clothes,' Jonathan commented, possessing only what he was wearing. 'I can't afford to buy any more.'

He wasn't sure what to do about his parents and Meddington, not wanting a police posse on his heels. He would have to let them know what he was doing shortly, although he did not want to disclose an address, should they achieve anything so unlikely.

It grew dark early, and started to rain and by the time they were closing with the coast the roads were virtually deserted. Although they had shared the driving, they were both tired, and knew Dogwood badly needed a break.

'We'll get off into a lane somewhere,' Peter decided. 'We're in the right area roughly. Can't do anything else in the dark.'

There was a full moon behind the rainclouds and as they

rounded a bend in the road it came out momentarily and shone on a wide sheet of water to seaward. Peter stopped the car and opened the window and they looked out. A smell of unmistakable ozone came on the cold wind, of weed and mud and things left by the tide; the unlikely, sad cries of estuary birds rose to the moon and were answered far away with a sad echo that reinforced the boys' instinctive feelings of loss, of not belonging. They were tired and hungry and could not find anything light-hearted to say at that moment. What they had done now did not appear very clever, although neither of them were so childish as to put this revelation into words.

'The next side road,' Peter said.

It appeared on the next bend, hiving off inland where the main road curved round to follow the water eastwards. Almost immediately there was a small driveway on the right, which Peter saw in the headlights before he had got up speed.

'How about this?'

It was a rough surface, arched over with trees, woods on the right and park palings on the left. Shortly there was a parking sign and a notice, 'Motorists stop here.'

'They're expecting us,' Peter said.

He pulled off obediently and switched off the engine. Jonathan wound down the window. Utter silence, a whiff of wet leaves, wet grass, cold wet soil. They were stiff and clammy, the hearse having no heater, and it was hard to make a move.

'The old nag'll want a walk round before we put him to bed,' Peter said.

Without the horse they could well have merely laid down and gone to sleep. As it was they had to unbox him, take him for a walk and a graze, unload the motor-bike, take out the partition, bed the now enlarged box down and put out feed and water (which Peter had brilliantly thought to bring in a five-gallon can). While Peter dressed the horse down before putting on his night rugs Jonathan brewed up

54

coffee on the camping stove and cleared out a sleeping place in the back of the hearse. It was a weird picnic, the moon shining fitfully between rain-heavy clouds, the horse nervously snatching at the grass and gazing around him with his bold, white-rimmed eyes. Wherever they were, there was nothing to disturb, no lights to be seen, only the flickering of skeleton leaves falling in the wind and the hooting of owls in some faraway wood.

Peter put Dogwood back in; then he came and sat with Jonathan in the back of the hearse to drink his coffee. They neither of them said anything, clamping cold hands round the hot mugs. Jonathan could not help thinking about Iris. Without Iris and her neurotic desire to give life, he would be in his uneventful bed at school now.

'Bloody girls,' he muttered.

'Oh, *girls*—' Peter agreed, in a voice of utmost disdain.

They got into their sleeping bags and went to sleep instantly.

Chapter 4

It was as if Jonathan's last waking thought was transmitted to his return of consciousness, for when he awoke he found himself staring straight into a pair of eyes, somewhat startled, that undoubtedly belonged to a girl. They were greenish and wide and beautiful, and the face (cool) and the body (slender and athletic) were all the ingredients of his dream-girl. Perhaps he was still dreaming ... the girl was sitting on a horse, leaning down, looking in through the window. What window? He got up on one elbow, alarmed, wondering where the hell he had got to, saw Peter, remembered, groaned. The girl laughed.

'Hell, I thought I'd found a pair of stiffs,' she said.

Cripes, but she was lovely! Jonathan slithered out of the back of the hearse in his sleeping-bag, remembered he had no pants on, so sat gawping, blinking, taking in the start of his new career. If this girl was part of the landscape, what a good place they had chosen.

'I was exercising across there—' The girl waved her arm towards the woods and parkland, 'And I saw this horse-box parked, so I came to look—'

'You live here?'

'Yes, on the farm down there.'

This was definitely the place to be, Jonathan decided.

He decided to wade straight in.

'We're looking for somewhere to keep the horse, and a barn or a loft or something to live in, just for a month or two, until the spring. Somewhere we can train—it's a chaser—'

Dogwood, conscious of another horse in the vicinity, whinnied shrilly.

'I thought you were taking it to be buried.' The girl smiled.

'Oh no. The hearse is coincidental.'

'There's a whole house down there,' The girl waved her stick vaguely over the park again. 'Like a palace. Going to be demolished. You could go and squat. There were squatters in it during the summer and no one said anything.'

Jonathan couldn't believe his luck.

'I'll show you if you like. You can drive down. I'll lead the way.'

Jonathan supposed, on the law of averages, he was owed some luck after the last week or two, and here it was. Bemused by such a visitation he got into his trousers while the girl went up the lane to open the gate. He threw his sleeping bag on top of Peter's head, got in the driving seat and eased the entourage back on to the lane. The girl was waiting for them a hundred yards up. The drive swung round here and entered the park between two impressive gateways, surmounted by stone lions. Ahead it ran over a ridge and disappeared into a tree-lined valley.

He drove through and stopped while the girl shut the gate behind them. She came back and stopped briefly beside Jonathan, 'My name's Pip, by the way. What's yours?'

'Jonathan. And that's Peter in the back.'

'Fine. Let's go.'

She put her horse into a canter and went briskly over the ridge, faster than Jonathan thought it prudent to drive, with the horsebox bumping and swaying behind. By the time they got to another gate she had opened it for him again, and waved him on; she then passed him at a gallop and by the time he reached the next hazard, a cattle-grid, she had jumped the adjoining stile and was disappearing into the woodland ahead. The drive entered the woodland and progressed down a shallow valley cleared back about thirty yards on either side, curving and mysterious with

57

very old trees rising high above on either side. In the early morning it was chill, cut off from the thin sun that was pulling out of the sea beyond, moisture dripping and oozing and trickling into the valley bottom. In the summer, Jonathan thought, it would be a magical place—with the girl. He changed down as the drive became more rutted.

'Am I dreaming?' Peter enquired sleepily from the back. 'What are you up to, Meredith?'

'Don't fret. Friendly native leading us to humble dwelling.'

'I don't believe it.'

'Go back to sleep.' Jonathan did not want to share the girl.

The drive slipped between heavy flanks of rhododendron then curved finally and came out into some paddocks which had been used for storing rough-hewn timber. Untidy stacks were scattered about and the ground was broken up by the heavy tractors and low-loaders that had worked there. Beyond, the house faced this area which had once, presumably, been its gardens, a vast, tattered mansion with a pillared portico up to the front door, gaunt windows twelve feet high, a stone balustrade crumbling across its skyline, manifesting ghosts and past glories as if made up for a film set, doomed, deserted, and incredibly desirable.

'Hey, we've got a house,' Jonathan said to Peter, as he drove up to the front door.

Peter sat up and looked out. 'Is that all?' he said.

Pip waited on her horse, non-committal.

'Will it do you?'

'Servants included?'

'Sorry. It's self-catering.'

'It's *amazing*. Are you serious?' Peter was not quite sure if he was properly awake.

'Well, no one else is using it. Seems a shame to waste it. It's going to be knocked down fairly soon. It's pretty far gone inside but it's dry and you could clean a room or two up and be quite comfortable, I would have thought.'

'Won't anyone mind?'

'My father might. He didn't like the squatters. But it isn't his, although he farms the estate. If you're polite and clean and call him sir he'll take to you. He's like that.'

'Oh.' They both knew a lot of people in the same mould. If being servile was a condition of tenancy, that was all right by them.

'We're not looking for something for nothing,' Jonathan said. 'We want to work, pay our way.'

'We've got to,' Peter pointed out. 'Not a matter of mere wanting.'

'There's not much work round here, not this time of year,' Pip said. 'I'll fish out the local paper if you want, see what there is, but I wouldn't be too hopeful. I'll come down later perhaps, see how you're getting on. If you decide to stay, that is.'

'I can't see us finding anything more suitable in a hurry. As long as we're allowed....'

'Fine then. I'll see you.'

She rode away, leaving the two boys bemused. Peter, slithering out of his sleeping-bag, said, 'I don't know what I was expecting, but it wasn't exactly a stately home. I thought a shed for the nag and the horse-box for us, as like as not.'

'You're not complaining?'

Peter grinned. 'Well, I might not like the wall-paper. I'm reserving judgement.'

He got dressed hastily and they walked up to the house front, up the steps to the vast front door, which was locked and immovable.

'Tradesmen's entrance, I think,' Peter said.

They walked round, across a terrace at the side and into a kitchen courtyard much littered with heaps of plaster and rubble and broken timber, presumably from inside the house. The doors were locked but a broken window gave easy access into a scullery. Peter tried the taps but there was no water.

'Snag number one.'

They walked through into a big kitchen, which was much knocked about and fouled and not at all inviting.

'The mod cons leave something to be desired,' Peter said.

'Who wants to live in a kitchen?' Jonathan enquired. 'Try the drawing-room. Think big.'

They went through a door and came out into the hall, which was vast and splendid with a floor of patterned tiles and a wide staircase rising up out of the middle of it, branching into two beneath a high arched window and disappearing out of sight in a plethora of gilded balustrade. The ceiling was dominated by an enormous chandelier, quite unvandalized, slightly cobwebby but still glittering impressively.

'That's more our style.' Jonathan approved of the hall. 'This has got class.'

'We could put Dogwood in here,' Peter said practically. 'Tiled floor, no windows for him to push his snout through.'

He tried the front door, and found it could be opened from the inside. 'Fine. He'd manage those steps all right.'

Jonathan looked out. There were only four steps up to the portico, and quite wide ones. He liked the idea of Dogwood entering by the front door and living with the chandelier.

'He might go up the stairs.'

'Yes. He's a nosy old devil. We'd have to fix a bar across.'

They explored the rooms that opened off on either side, the drawing room that gave on to the side terrace, and opposite a dining room. Both had broken windows and large holes in the floors, which had been used for firewood. Behind the drawing-room, with windows to the terrace and the kitchen yard at the back, was a smaller room, a morning-room or study, which looked more promising—

cleaner, at least, and with a floor. The ceiling had fallen down but the windows were whole. There was a beautiful marble fireplace with carved ladies on either side, scantily clad, and a grate of reasonable proportions.

'You could cook on that all right,' Peter said.

It was weird, coming to terms with this place as somewhere to live for the next six months. After the first reconnaissance it seemed prudent to attend to Dogwood first, who was getting restive in his cramped quarters and trying to kick the ramp down.

'He'll have to be exercised before we do anything else,' Peter said. 'I suppose I ought to do it. You could move in, I suppose.'

Jonathan reckoned that would take all of five minutes, with their skeleton gear.

'I'll clean the room up a bit. Okay.'

They had a broom in Dogwood's kit, for Dogwood was lavishly provided for, unlike his grooms. When Peter rode away Jonathan mucked out their proposed living room, using Dogwood's shovel and broom, and made a table under the window with planks and two empty oil drums, and put their camping stove and lamp on it, complete with the tin-opener, matches, two plates, two mugs, frying-pan and kettle that made up their gear. The box of hastily gathered food he shoved underneath, and the mattress and sleeping bags he flung in another corner. A fire would have made the place more homely, but although there was plenty of wood around he had nothing to cut it up with. A water supply was a necessity, and he went outside to see what he could find.

None of the taps, inside or out, worked. He reckoned they could deflect rainwater off the roof into a waterbutt, should they possess such a luxury, but while he was studying the drains he came across a well in the corner of the kitchen courtyard, obviously long derelict but at least not filled in. It had a wooden cover over it and a primitive sort of windlass arrangement, much rusted and rotted, to wind up a bucket, but no bucket. He lifted the lid off and peered in. The hole was very old and clammy but smelled just like a well should, earthy but clean. He dropped a pebble down, and from far away, after a considerable pause, it sent up the echo of a tiny splash. Highly satisfactory, he thought ... apart from the fact that they had only one bucket—and that was Dogwood's—and no rope to lower it on.

It occurred to him fairly rapidly that they lacked nearly everything that went to make up the normal necessities of living. Aside from armchairs, colour TV and a music centre, they lacked the nitty-gritty like saw and hammer, screwdriver, gum-boots, washing-up bowl, pot-scrubber, clothes, scissors, soap, beds, string, etc. Whatever he went to do he found himself frustrated by the lack of wherewithal: nothing with which to turn timber into firewood, nothing to fix a bar across the stairs with to discourage Dogwood's explorations, no way to obtain the water to put in the kettle to make a cup of tea (Dogwood having inconsiderately drunk all that Peter had brought). He looked for rope in vain, for utensils, for basics. By the time Peter came back, he had only discovered how much they lacked.

'Oh, come off it, a house—and the well—that's not bad before breakfast.' Peter on his return was far more optimistic. He positively glowed with well-being. Jonathan put it down to a bracing ride but as Peter unsaddled in the drive he said, 'I went past the farm and that girl was putting her horse away, so I stopped, civilized like, to ask if it was okay to ride through and where could I go and where could I not, and she said would I like a cup of coffee, so I said yes and she said put the nag in here for ten minutes, so I did and she took me in and we had coffee sitting by the Aga and very nice it was too. I reckon we've turned up trumps here.'

Jonathan could have hit him.

'Big deal.'

Peter got the message.

'Well, it made sense—not just to gallop all over the place without asking. Only being well brought up. The country code and what we learnt in the Pony Club and all that.'

'And the girl and the coffee.'

'Oh, yeah, well, bonus points, admitted.'

Jonathan felt ridiculously angry but tried not to show it too much. It was crazy but he felt jealous of Peter. He had never been quite so struck by a bird at first sight as by this one. Perhaps sex with Iris had stimulated his instincts, or being a homeless reject made coffee by an Aga desirable out of all proportion. No, coffee without the girl would have aroused a much milder jealousy than that which he now had considerable trouble in suppressing. Peter, not such a bonehead as he looked, became kind and conciliatory and said congratulatory things about Jonathan's home-making, and Jonathan then felt embarrassed by having revealed such pettiness, and made amends by unloading the straw off the top of the hearse and humping it into Dogwood's new quarters.

'Pip said it wouldn't matter, putting him in here. The whole place is to be bulldozed in the spring.'

Peter's casual use of the girl's name was best ignored. Jonathan flung the bale of straw bodily through the front door.

'When we've done this I want to go and get my motorbike,' he said. 'I don't like leaving it up there in the lane. It'll get knocked off.'

'Yeah, fine. I'll stay with Dogwood. He'll take a bit to settle, I imagine. He's a bit bonkers, his routine all knocked for six, and all his friends disappeared.'

Horses were gregarious animals, Jonathan knew, and the change in Dogwood's life would upset him, high-mettled beast that he was, for a while. His new loose-box, even with straw on the floor, looked unlikely even to Jonathan. To Dogwood, coaxed up to the front door, it was obviously amazing, to be explored with fastidious care. He walked round like a paying sightseer, nibbling the bannisters, goggling at the chandelier, pawing at the tiles. Peter gave him his feed and sat on the stairs, prepared to sit in indefinitely.

'What we want is a big load of straw in here. Deep litter him and take some of the echo out of the place. We'll go up to the farm again later and see if we can buy some.' He hung a haynet on a light fitting that stuck out of the wall. There were shutters over the windows on either side of the front door, but the wintry sunshine peered in from the fanlights over the door and from the high landing window at the top of the stairs and filled the strange stable with moving shadows as the horse wheeled about.

'You could take the water-carrier and fill it at the farm on the way back,' Peter suggested. 'Until we get the well working.'

A gesture of understanding, Jonathan sensed, meaning your go to chat up Pip. He took the can nevertheless, and set off with it back the way they had come in the hearse earlier.

No one had knocked off his bike and it stood where it had been unloaded from the horsebox. Jonathan started it up and rode back with the water-carrier balanced in front of him, and turned up the track for the farm, which skirted the wood to the right and dropped down into a cosy hollow where the old buildings huddled, all pleasantly mellow and harmonious, not a tin roof or silo to be seen. Suffolk farms are more aesthetic than most, Jonathan decided, looking as if they belonged to people who liked the look of them rather than investing in modern methods; perhaps Pip's father was farmer to whoever owned the estate, not the owner of these lush acres. He actually had his hens out pecking and not in a battery shed, and two carthorses grazing in a small paddock. Old-fashioned, Jonathan thought, picturing side-whiskers and a pipe ... and drove round the end of a straw barn into the path of a sharp-featured, fortyish man with an undeniably contemporary ski-ing jacket keeping the wind from his snappy frame, and an unwelcoming glint in his eye that immediately torpedoed visions of coffee in the kitchen by the Aga.

Jonathan halted and turned off his engine politely.

The man waited coldly for him to explain his business, not making it easy.

'Is there a tap where I could fill this can, sir? I've got a horse that needs watering.' As a farmer, he might be more sympathetic to the watering of stock, rather than of humans.

'Are you the gipsy with the horse my daughter met earlier?'

'There are two of us and we're not gipsies.' Not by birth, only by inclination.

'What are you up to, trailing round the countryside with a horse?'

'We're looking for jobs.' A fine, old-fashioned, upstanding ambition.

'Why the horse?'

'We're training it, sir. It's ours. It's a chaser.'

'It's no place for jobs out here, you know. Not this time of year. In the summer perhaps.'

He was softening, perhaps because of all the 'sirs'. He nodded his head to indicate the water-tap and said, 'Help yourself.' He hesitated. 'See how it goes. I'll be keeping an eye on you. You're not inviting any friends down, I hope?'

'No, sir.'

'Last summer we had a load of layabouts, you know—long hair, half-naked. They smoked pot. The police had to come. We don't want any of that again.'

'We don't smoke, either of us.'

'Very well then.'

Jonathan filled the water-can and drove back to their ruin, smarting at the injustice of Peter meeting Pip and himself meeting Pip's father. At least, the confrontation had given their squat the semblance of respectability. They had permission, if grudging. When he got back he made a pot of tea and they had a sort of breakfast—bread and marmalade and tea—and decided that Jonathan should go out and buy a bit more food and something to cut wood with, and a local paper for the job situation, and have a general snout round.

'It's all a bit too good to be true so far,' Peter said.

'Are you coming?'

'I think it would be a bit stupid to leave Dogwood, just at the moment.'

Jonathan had visions of Pip calling and them sitting on the stairs, talking....

He put his gear on and went out to the bike.

It wasn't bad to be astride the old engine again and a blast of near eighty miles an hour up the main road cleared his blues slightly. He took a road to seaward and found himself riding over sandy commonland, the ground a tawny tangle of bracken and heather and dried out gorse, heavily wooded in Forestry Commission patterns with pines and birch—splendid riding country, he noted with satisfaction. Or was it just his luck if Peter got the training job, riding out with the delectable Pip every day, while he slaved away as lavatory attendant, garage-hand or farm labourer? After a few miles the road swooped up over a ridge and the trees parted to reveal the pearly shimmer of the winter sea ahead. Low sandy cliffs crumbled away below to miles of gritty beach. Jonathan rode his bike off over the turfy grass to the cliff edge and sat looking down, feeling soothed. There was nobody in sight, no traffic, not even a ship. He liked seaside like that. He could have said it reminded him of Sivota, but the thought was like a needle jab. He thought of Pip being Iris on that honey-smelling turf, and the needle bit deep, bringing him up short. Christ, he was getting unbalanced! He had only spoken two or three sentences to the girl, only set eyes on her about three hours ago ... she had a father like a prison governor, and he must take a grip on himself. The idea of running away with Peter was to find freedom and peace of

66

mind, not to put his head into the same snare he had been caught in already.

He remembered he was out to buy food, not admire the landscape, and rode on looking for civilization. It was fairly scattered in this part of the world. The nearest town was some six miles farther on, a rather classy seaside place with Copper Kettle type restaurants and art galleries and no welcoming smell of fish and chips. He was damned hungry, he realized, and parked the bike, intent on selfish stoking of the inner man. He found a cafe and pigged happily for half an hour which improved his view of life considerably. He then bought a small axe, some rope at a yacht chandlers, a fair selection of food, six Mars bars and six cans of beer.

When he got home, Peter was grooming Dogwood and said no one had been near all morning.

They did not see the girl again for several days, although her father called one dusking afternoon and asked them some headmasterish sort of questions about their intentions. Fortunately he was distracted by his admiration for Dogwood, standing under the chandelier in a shaft of wintry sunset from the landing window and looking every inch a Grand National winner. Having plenty of time, they had worked on him devotedly since their arrival, and the man obviously knew his horses. He introduced himself as Anstruther, no title, and was slightly embarrassed by inspecting them—'But we've had trouble here, you understand. I don't want to be caught again.' They were polite and affable and called him sir again, and his prickles retreated and he agreed that they could have as much straw as they wanted if they collected it in the hearse, and buy their hay and oats off him.

'And clear off like good chaps if the demolition firm moves in, then nobody'll mind. They aren't due till the spring, mind you.'

He did not know of any jobs going. The ones in the local paper they enquired about were already taken. They had enough ready money for about three weeks' living and feeding Dogwood, and then only Jonathan's allowance in the bank, which he was not too keen on using.

'I don't want to sponge on my parents. All right when I'm doing the right thing, but not when I've hived off like this.'

'We've just got to find something,' Peter said, 'Or go on the dole, I suppose. But you need a proper address for the dole. And it won't keep a horse in training anyway. I don't think you're supposed to keep a racehorse on the dole.'

'What you do with the dole money is your own affair surely? You don't blurt out you've got a racehorse when you're standing in the dole queue, woodenhead. Perhaps we ought to sign on.'

It was three days before the Oxford entrance examinations were due to start and Jonathan was progressively edgy as the date approached, feeling that he could—if so inclined—still renounce his errant ways and go back to Meddington like a good boy and return to his proper vocation. Conventional and obedient by nature, what he was doing now frightened him if he lay awake at night on the hard mattress and considered his future. He didn't actually have one any more. It was a new sensation, the total freedom that now faced him, having all his life slavishly followed his academic curriculum without question in the safe knowledge that he was going to get a well-paid job in his father's concern in the city when he was through. Peter did not have this sense of the carpet having been pulled out from under him, because his way ahead had always been racketty. Becoming a jockey, his long-held ambition, was notoriously a non-starter in the security stakes. Peter had always expected disappointment, unemployment, frustration and lack of money as a matter of course. His present situation was more or less the norm. But a ride in the Grand National was going to make it all worthwhile to his cracked way of thinking, whereas for Jonathan there was no ultimate goal, only the momentary comfort of avoiding present difficulties. It made him feel bad when he thought about it seriously.

More practically, he was desperately short of clothes and had no riding gear, boots, or decent anorak and decided that he would have to make a visit home to collect some necessities.

'I could bring a whole load of stuff if I take the hearse—we've got camping furniture in the barn, and crockery and saucepans and suchlike, not to mention tools and a big axe and a wheelbarrow. We've got about six of everything at home—nobody's going to miss a few items.'

'What if you come face to face with Mummy?'

'I won't idiot. Say I go Friday—she's always in court all day Friday.'

'What, sentencing people to prison?'

'Yeah, her JP lark. And Dad'll be in town. I needn't meet anybody if I'm careful.'

'Only Iris the mother-figure.'

'Oh, my God, I'll make sure I miss her! Apart from the clothes, I can get most things we want out of the yard.'

'Well, its's not a bad idea,' Peter conceded. Mention of the wheelbarrow swayed him: life was hard without a wheelbarrow.

'I could have a bath if Iris isn't there.'

Simple things now had an unexpected appeal. 'Yeah, bring one back, and a hot water system to go with it, and a couple of spring beds with mattresses and electric blankets.'

'Electricity! Yes, what bliss!'

'And a breadknife.'

'I'll go then. It'll save a lot of money, getting the gear we want—as much as the cost of petrol, at any rate. And it can all go back when we get jobs and leave this place—in the spring or whenever. It won't be stealing. I'll leave an explanatory note.'

69

Afterwards, thinking about it, Jonathan wondered if he acted out of some deep psychological desire to be apprehended and persuaded back to Meddington. It was risky, after all. Sometimes his father stayed at home or his mother might miss a Friday. He could have gone later the next week, when the first important examination date had gone past, but he had a compulsion to go at once, while his options were still open, a great longing to go home. It was not far, a mere forty miles.

It took less than an hour in the hearse (traffic tended to give way out of respect—they had noticed this on the way down, even with the horsebox stuck on behind). There was a half mile drive across parkland into Ravenshall Court, but Jonathan chose the back farm road which led into the stableyard at the back of the house. He arrived at half past ten in the morning, and left the hearse in the tractor barn out of sight, just outside the yard gate. Even if Jim the groom saw him it would not matter, he had decided in advance, for he was unlikely to take more than a passing interest, the domestic affairs of the family not being his province. Iris was the danger. He did not *at all* want to meet Iris.

He got out of the hearse and peered tentatively round the corner of the barn into the yard. The familiarity of the scene speared him with a sentimental pang of longing for what he was missing; it was weird to feel he had no place here any more. He was now the prodigal son, out on his ear.

'At least they can't deny me my underpants,' he thought defiantly.

All was well in that both his mother's and father's cars were missing, the garage doors wide open. The Land-Rover was out too, which meant Jim was out of the way. Jonathan filled the hearse rapidly with the gear he wanted out of the barn, the camping-stuff and Peter's wheelbarrow, a handy pair of gumboots, a sledge-hammer, axe and saw. He went to the tack-room and got his racing helmet and hunting cap, in case, stowed them in the hearse and got the spare house key out from behind the linseed oil where it was habitually kept. (He had only got into the tack-room because he knew where the key was, under the rainwater butt). He then approached the back of the house, on tenterhooks for Iris, feeling exactly like a burglar.

The dogs recognized him and made no undue commotion as he let himself into the kitchen. There were no other signs of life. Everything was tidy, all the washing-up put away, the boiler humming softly. The house was deliciously warm, the carpets deep and soft to his stockinged feet. He had forgotten how civilized his home was and went through into the hall sensuously enjoying the familiar surroundings—until he remembered that he was in the act of throwing it all over for McNair's bloody race-horse and central heating was no part of his future any longer. Iris had usurped his place ... where was she? Halfway up the stairs Jonathan stood and listened, but the place was quite silent. The stairs creaked. He knew exactly where, but it was impossible to avoid every spot. A pale November sunlight irradiated the spacious Tudor hall below him, burnishing the oak panelling and the carvings on the staircase, worn smooth by centuries of hands; every chiselled leaf and embellishment was well-known to him, every knot and crack and wormhole. It was a part of him, this house; its beauty never failed to move him. It was crazy to be cutting himself off from it, he knew it and could change nothing, the way he felt.

He went into his room and pulled his holiday bag out from under the bed and packed it with the clothes he wanted, putting in some flash stuff as well as working gear, in case he was destined to lead in the winner of the Grand National or land a job in a menswear shop. When he had done that the temptation to have a bath overcame him, so he fetched some hot towels from the airing cupboard and turned on the taps in the nearest bathroom. His mother's

Labrador came up and lay on the floor against the hot pipes, waving his tail in friendly fashion, and Jonathan undressed and lowered himself into the scorching water with a sigh of bliss. He left the door open so that he could hear if a car came into the yard or a door slammed somewhere, and lay thinking how wonderful baths were when they were rationed to one a fortnight or so. Having one every day completely obscured the luxury value. It was stupid to bathe out of habit. If this was the only bath he was destined to have until next spring he determined to make the best of it, and sprinkled in his mother's bottled relaxing salts and his father's 'Freshfoam' for good measure, and lay back with his eyes shut in a cloud of steam and bubbles.

'Hullo, Jonathan.'

He must have dozed off. Iris was sitting on the bathroom chair regarding him complacently, smiling and idly stroking the dog. Jonathan, panicking, instinctively made to submerge, but controlled himself in time not to make a complete fool of himself, and lay blinking, speechless.

'I wondered who it was, hearing the water running.' She did not seem surprised. 'Are you going to stay?'

'No, I'm not.'

'Are you going back to Meddington?'

'No.'

'They're all in a frightful stew about you.'

'Serves them right.'

'I'm sorry they were so hard on you. I didn't mean to get you into trouble.'

Jonathan could not credit the girl, and found no words to answer her with. She radiated complacent satisfaction, rounded and smiling, her eyes grown soft and sleepy like a fat cat's, her once brittle, crackly hair glowing and looping in golden trails over her shoulders.

'I am so happy,' she said.

Jonathan reached for the bath-towel, thinking 'Bully for

72

you' but not saying a word. He felt sorely put out, the indignation that Iris always aroused in him welling up through his steaming pores, the bitterness of his exile flooding him with self-pity—no soft carpets, hot water or sirloin steak, but hard graft all the way to Aintree (they had never spoken of what might happen after Aintree; their ambitions finished there). And Iris growing fat both physically and spiritually in the plush surroundings of Ravenshall, like a cuckoo in the nest, nurtured by her surrogate mother, his own flint-faced mummy who had pushed him out splat on the cold floor.... Jonathan huddled deep into the Harrods towels, making the most of his moment of luxury....

'Poor Jonathan,' Iris said softly.

He knew then what was going to happen. He would go down fighting but his situation was hopeless. It was going to be Greece all over again, he could see by the look in Iris's eyes.

'Where's my mother?' he asked.

'She's gone to court.'

'And my father?'

'Gone to London.'

'Why did you do that to me? Tell all those lies?'

'Because I wanted a baby so badly.'

'You could easily have used someone else. You might have guessed how they would react.'

'But I wanted it to be yours.'

She got up and came and laid her head on his shoulder and put her arms round him. Wrapped in the bath-towel he could not either fend her off or encourage her, the situation in a nutshell. Even while he felt his desire for her rising he knew he loathed her, and himself equally.

'Why do you take everything so seriously?' she murmured. 'I've never asked you to love me, have I?'

'What are you doing now?'

'I mean *love*, not just sex.'

'They're supposed to be all of a piece.'

73

'If you want it for posterity. You know I love you, but I've never asked—never supposed—expected—you would marry me.'

'Thank Christ for that.'

'Well, stop being so old-fashioned and love me not for posterity but just for what is called physical gratification.'

After all, he could not imagine anyone else he knew turning down such an offer. He trailed back to his bedroom with her, bemused, amazed—as ever—by girls in general and Iris in particular. What the hell ... he was going to get precious little comfort in the months ahead! And even as he took Iris in his arms on the bed he thought of the delectable, skinny green-eyed Pip back in Suffolk, and the ridiculous confusions in his intellect as to what the whole love machine actually meant, was about, foundered in the flowering of his desire as Iris came into the embrace of the damp bath-towel. She was quite right really, and he was all wrong, because at the actual moment of impact it did not really matter a damn who it was.

But before, and afterwards, it was all hopeless.

He was back to confusion again, drifting on a cloud of lovely, wrung-out well-being when the sound of a car on the gravel drive came to his ears, and his mother's Labrador went cantering down the landing with an ominous air of welcome.

Jonathan surfaced, incredulous.

'You said she'd gone to court!'

'I thought—'

He'd forgotten what a liar Iris was. As long as she got what she wanted—

'Jesus! Get out!' he hissed. 'Get dressed, for God's sake!'

His clothes were in the bathroom.

'Go and fetch them—hurry! And go down and keep her in the kitchen—'

But by the time Iris was presentable and Jonathan was

half into his jeans, Mrs Meredith's voice could be heard in the hall, 'Iris! Iris, dear, I'm back. I'll bring you up a coffee.'

Being a woman of action, she was already on her way. Sandy the Labrador, preceding her, naturally led the way to Jonathan's bedroom. Jonathan kicked his packed hold-all under the bed, grabbed the bath-towel off the covers and dived after it. Iris had a brief moment to pull the duvet straight and the presence of mind to fling herself full-length and grab a paperback off the bedside table, which she opened as if she was reading.

'Whatever are you doing in Jonathan's room?'

Jonathan saw his mother's feet appear alongside. The bed was a Jacobean four-poster and had plenty of living-space underneath and a good tapestry valence to hide him. As long as Sandy ignored him and Iris told enough of her practised lies he stood a chance. But his heart was thudding painfully. If she found him he would not be able to escape again. At that moment the bare room back in the ruined mansion with its pathetic furnishings seemed the equivalent of paradise.

'I was just looking through his books,' Iris said, sounding quite calm. She was well-practised in deceit.

'What a strange one to choose!'

Jonathan wondered what it was, trying to think back to what he had had last holiday. As far as he could remember it was a handbook on motor-bike maintenance.

'You're not that bored, are you? I should think Jessica's books would suit you better than Jonathan's. Why don't you look in her room?'

'Yes, I will.'

'Meddington hasn't rung, I suppose?'

'No.'

'His first exam is tomorrow. I really did think—do think—he will turn up for it.'

'I don't,' Iris said. 'Meddington is awful, you know.'

'He never thought so. I know you did. Even so, he can

leave as soon as the exam is over. If only we knew where he was!'

'He'll be all right.'

'Of course he'll be all right. He just won't get into Oxford. That's what concerns me.'

His mother sounded as if she was suffering from a slight superfluity of Iris. The stupid girl was still lying on the bed, making no effort to lead his mother away so that he could escape. It occurred to him that if the child took after its mother it would turn out a pain.

If only he hadn't stopped for a bath! He could have been away by now and laughing.

Iris said, 'Does getting into Oxford matter that much?'

'My dear girl, we did not spend all that money on the boy's education to have him drop out just when it matters. I'm afraid if he does not take that examination he will completely forfeit any claims to a place in his father's firm—we honestly could not support him any more if he gives so little consideration to his future. Of course it matters! Life is very competitive, you know.'

'It's my fault really,' Iris said.

'I think he must take the blame. He knew—knows now—exactly what he is doing and what the consequences are. Now come on, Iris, you can't moon around here all day. Drink this coffee and come downstairs. I wouldn't really be surprised if he were to walk in. Wherever he is, he must be frightfully short of clothes.'

With that penetrating remark she retreated and Jonathan heard her going downstairs. He crawled out and bagged the coffee before Iris started on it.

'You just egg her on,' he complained. 'I wonder you didn't ask her her opinion of me so that I could have got the full benefit lying there. Not that I don't know, anyway.'

'Aren't you going back then?'

'No, I'm not.'

He pushed the empty coffee cup at her. 'Take this

downstairs and keep her in the kitchen while I get out. Go in the kitchen and slam the door so that I can hear, and I'll go out by the passage door into the garden.'

'Goodbye. Come back soon.'

Iris smiled at him, like the Cheshire cat. She really was mental, Jonathan thought, having turned from a neurotic bag of nerves into this cow-like earth-figure, all her spots and traumas exchanged for a calm radiance he found hard to credit. She always brought out the worst in him; he was rude to her and bullied her, and she just smiled, as she was smiling now. In the past she had wept. But she never argued, complained, nagged, got indignant. She made him feel a complete rat.

She kissed him and departed.

He got out safely, the house being so large that there was little difficulty. He skirted the back yard which was overlooked by the kitchen, and came back to the hearse via the kitchen garden and a corner of the park. He booted his bag in the back, got in and set off for what he now thought of as home. He felt very disturbed and felt he had paid dearly for a few material comforts. As he drove he kept hearing his mother's voice saying, 'Life is very competitive, you know.' Having been acutely geared to the rat-race all his eighteen years, he found it harder than most to drop out and watch the rats go racing on. Peter, for example, had never been brought up to expect riches and status. He might have discovered his own special rat-race in wanting to succeed at being a jump-jockey, but the path there was untrammelled by the sort of philosophical and psychological pressures the Meddington society was so practised in. If he turned up at Meddington tomorrow for his examination he would be back in the fold, society approved. And if he did not, he was subjecting himself to a lifetime of lost opportunities—certainly in his parents' eyes. It was difficult to go against the weight of disapproval he felt himself to bear.

'But I bloody well will,' he said to the red traffic lights

that tempered his progress. He had always been a disappointment to his ambitious mother, so he might as well go ahead and make a good job of it.

'Yeah, well, the Grand National is blooming competitive too, you know,' Peter commented when Jonathan told him of his day's adventures. Jonathan held back, at first, about Iris, but when they were eating baked beans on toast by the light of the expensive Meredith camping lamps, lolling in equally expensive cushioned camping chairs in front of their blazing fire, newly-chopped logs piled high to last the evening, he told him, somewhat indirectly, what had happened.

'Cripes, they *throw* themselves at you, Meredith, and you're nothing special to look at! What's your secret, for heaven's sake? In the *bath*, like in a bloody film—'

'Not in the bath, idiot—I got out, didn't I? Anyway it's only Iris—who else throws themselves? I wish they blooming well would....' He was thinking of Pip throwing herself, had been thinking about her ever since he got back, actually, steamed up by his encounter with Iris, not daring to ask Peter if he had seen her.

'That Melissa Jones—don't you remember? She thought you were fantastic, she told me so.'

'That was only a joke, wasn't it? She married someone. Said I was too young. Rich enough, but too young and she couldn't wait.'

'No one'll ever throw themselves at me for my riches.'

'Nor me either after tomorrow, if I don't turn up at Meddington.'

'You're not going to, are you?'

'No.'

'I mean, you could, if you want. I wouldn't want to be the cause of your being cut off without a penny or whatever it is millionaires like your pa do.'

'No. I'm staying.'

Peter ladled out another dollop of baked beans from the saucepan in the hearth. The kettle, balanced on the bars of the grate, was beginning to sizzle encouragingly.

'You'll get by,' Peter said, 'Without a lousy degree. It's not just that your mother means, I think. It's you not wanting what they think is so important, you thinking differently. Your mother was never a one to disagree with, even when it was just the Pony Club.'

'No.'

'Perhaps she'll go all soft over the baby, all loving—grannyish, and all will be forgiven. Funny, you having a baby. Don't you think about it?—you know, feel all—er—'

'What?'

Peter considered. 'Well, if it was me, I'd feel a bit pleased with myself, I think.'

'It's very common. Much cleverer not to have one.' Jonathan could honestly say he had no feelings about the baby at all, other than feelings of rage and the perennial grievance of feeling hard done by. When Peter thought that strange, he got worried, wondering if he was unnatural. He was going to be very glad when the next twelve hours were through, being on edge about going back to Meddington. He could still get back in time, on his motor-bike, up till eight o'clock the following morning.

When they went to bed, (on their new camping beds complete with mattresses and pillows) he lay miserably listening to the wind in the trees outside, in two minds as to whether to get dressed and leap on his motor-bike. Whichever course he took, it was failure of a kind. But he stuck it out and in the morning, while Peter did Dogwood, he lit the fire and sat crouched over the hearth, turning rashers of bacon in the frying pan, cold and stiff and demoralized, and the time crept past until it was too late. Peter came back and made the tea. He poured it out and held up his mug.

'Here's to you, Meredith, you're a free man at last.'

And then it got better, with no going back, and Jonathan thawed out and decided to go down to Southaven, the town down the coast, and sign on for the dole and see if he could find a job.

'I'd like to do something zombie for a bit, like digging holes.' He wanted something physical, to make him tired and stop him thinking.

'You could do the Dogwood bit, if you like. Or we can take it in turns.'

Doing Dogwood did not look very zombie-ish to Jonathan, what he had seen of it, and he declined.

'I'll send a letter to my mother and tell her I'm not coming back for a bit. So she knows I'm alive and doesn't get a search-party out. I'll send it via some people I know in Scotland, so the postmark won't give us away, and then that's that.'

He got on the bike and went to Southaven. It was raining and cold. The dole people were horrible and fobbed him off, telling him to sign on where he lived before, but he would not give them his former address, and they got suspicious and the whole morning got tangled into a misunderstanding. He looked for jobs and followed up two: one for a barman and one for a filing-clerk, but both were said to be filled. As he wanted neither of them he was not particularly disappointed. He tried to think of things he could do that other people couldn't, and could not think of anything. The only possibility that emerged from the newspaper columns was 'Tutor for O-level Maths and English'. Although unqualified, he was fresh from the scene. He rode back along the cliffs to try and cheer himself up, but the sea was flattened by a continuous rain, the sky grey and featureless; old sodden newspapers blew along the beach. The rain was getting in and the bike was short of petrol. If he couldn't get a job he would have to sell it, which thought depressed him still farther.

Thoroughly fed up, he turned for home. His address, as given to the dole, was Mallow End Manor, but the girl had laughed and said, 'Nobody lives there! It's fallen down.' It was home nevertheless. It was dusk and their new lamps shone brightly in the windows as he powered up the drive. His headlamps picked up a car squatting by the front door, a battered Mini. He recognized it as Pip's, and his stomach gave a lurch. He thought of her having been there all day with Peter while he had been scraping around for jobs, and his jealousy flared up miserably.

He could not understand why this girl, whom he had scarcely spoken to, had the power to provoke such stupid feelings in him.

He went in through the back kitchen, trying to feel civilized, and through the hall where Dogwood had settled complacently beneath the great chandelier, hock-deep in straw and looking quite at home. Peter had fed him, and he was occupied happily with a large haynet, and only cocked an ear at Jonathan's passing. Jonathan could hear Peter laughing. He opened the door, blinking in the greenish flare of the lamps. Pip was standing over the frying-pan at the makeshift bench under the window, turning some concoction over with the fish-slice, frowning with concentration, and Peter was cutting bread and chatting away nineteen to the dozen.

'Hey, you've timed it well,' he said amiably to Jonathan.

'Lucky I did enough for three,' Pip said. 'He said you'd arrive if there was food in the offing.' She glanced up at Jonathan with a smile that quite dispersed his irritability. 'Cooking's not my thing, really, but with luck it's edible.'

'That's great. I'm starving.'

He was too, but suddenly felt a whole lot better, included into this cosy domestic scene. The room looked much improved with Pip in it, positively homely, the camping table and chairs pulled up in front of the fire with some decent Meredith cutlery and plates set out and some cans of beer winking in the firelight.

'She fetched us some eggs, so I thought it was worth asking her to stay and cook them,' Peter said. 'A clever move, you must admit.'

'You might live to regret it,' Pip said.

She was no disappointment, Jonathan decided, pleasure overcoming his day's miseries. He started to strip off his motor-bike gear, and Peter threw some more logs on the fire.

'How did it go?'

'It didn't really. No dole until they decide that I really live at this address, and two jobs—I went to see but they were both taken. Said they were anyway. There are one or two things in the paper might fit.'

'Well, Pip's come up trumps—something just up our street. Let's get dished up, and we'll talk about it.'

'It's a job at a stables, point-to-pointers,' Pip said. 'Riding out, schooling, grooming, general dogsbody. Not too far away—five miles. Present fellow packed it in to go to a National Hunt place. That's why I came down, because I thought it might suit you—one of you.'

'That's terrific! If one of us had the job, for cash, and the other did the nag, we'd get by.'

Pip divided up a vast omelette into three and tipped it out of the pan on to their plates. They opened the beer cans and toasted themselves cheerfully. The possibility of such a job put a different complexion on the day altogether; Jonathan wondered if it was a bit too good to be true. Shovelling in the omelette—God, he really was starving!— he tried to think of the drawbacks. The main drawback was that whoever had the job would be out of range of Pip all day, while whoever stayed behind and did Dogwood stood a good chance of running into her at any time perhaps riding out with her, even taking her to the pub for a beer at lunchtime. . . . Jonathan, aware of her proximity, her knee almost brushing his under the table—and Peter's too, the table being so small, but that was beside the point—tried to work out as he ate how to wangle getting the Dogwood job, and Peter the paid groom's, without appearing to care which he did, not to make it obvious . . . to be nonchalant . . . God, he really did want to be around her all day! The thought of it made him sweat. With Peter being five miles away for eight hours or so, he stood a fantastic chance of getting the advantage. She looked marvellous in the firelight, although she was only dressed in jeans and gumboots and a muddy anorak. She wasn't beautiful, as he had first thought, being too thin and angular; the bones in her face showed too much and she had a rather shy, slightly nervous way of looking. Perhaps that was why he was so drawn to her, as the out-going, self-confident ones always frightened him; she seemed a quiet person by nature, and not at all a sexually-aware flaunter like the mob at school. She was interested in Dogwood, and impressed by his National pretensions.

'Who is going to ride him?'

'I am,' Peter said.

'God, you're brave!'

Peter looked genuinely surprised at this. 'Oh no. Not on Dogwood, anyway. He's a super jumper.'

Mark to Peter, Jonathan thought. He would love Pip to think him brave and tell him so, but in fact he had no ambition to ride in the National, even on a good jumper. Point-to-points were one thing, the Grand National another altogether. He knew his limitations.

'I suppose if you're the trainer, then Jonathan will take the job,' Pip said, as if it was fait accompli.

'I don't mind doing the training,' Jonathan said, rather more quickly than was wise. 'It's only riding out, after all, and stable work, and Peter knows more about schooling jumpers than I do.'

'It will be awfully boring, training one horse,' Peter said. 'Riding by yourself every day. He needs a hell of a lot of work, Dogwood. About three hours suits him—he never got enough back at the yard. He's so nosey and lively, he gets bored very quickly.'

'I wouldn't mind,' Jonathan said. 'It might combine quite well if I were to get this O-level cramming job.'

'Yeah, but if they want a jockey I can't ride races for them. I'm a professional.'

Only amateur riders could ride in point-to-points. Jonathan had ridden in several and now found the qualification an embarrassment.

To his relief Pip said, 'They don't want a jockey. The owner's son rides them in races. It's only the work.' She smiled her rather shy, enchanting smile in Jonathan's direction and said, 'I'm sure you'd suit them beautifully.'

Peter said, 'Well, if he prefers doing Dogwood, leave him be. The old devil drives me round the bend. I'll have the job—if they'll have me, that is.'

'Fine,' Pip said. 'You're both super-qualified by their standards. They'll be terribly pleased I've found them someone.'

'How will you travel in?' Jonathan asked, feeling extremely pleased with himself. 'You could borrow my motor-bike if you like.'

'He can travel in with me,' Pip said.

'How do you mean?' Jonathan asked.

'I work there. He can come in my Mini. And come home with me. It's no problem.'

Afterwards Jonathan supposed if he had had the presence of mind he could have thought of some way of switching his intentions and getting the job even then but at the time he was completely thrown by Pip's revelation. While he was still gawping the conversation switched to something else and the occasion never arose again. He might have done it by admitting privately to Peter how much he wanted to be where Pip was, but that he could not bring himself to do. The last person he wanted to know about his susceptibilities was Peter. He was lumbered, and Peter was to spend all day in the girl's company, and he in the horse's.

In some perverse way he thought he had got his just deserts. He had behaved badly over Iris, and this was a squaring of the account. He accepted it, but it did not make his future look any the brighter and it was with a feeling very close to despair that he watched Peter depart in the Mini the next morning, and turned to set about the serious training of Dogwood.

Chapter 5

While Peter pursued his relationship with Pip, so did Jonathan with Dogwood, gloomily, stubbornly, relentlessly. If the whole point of the exercise was to get round the Grand National course in the spring, so they bloody well would, or not for want of being fit and able. He had no other goal to work towards, neither examinations nor a love-life, so the horse it was. He rode him out for three hours every day, through rainstorms, gale and snow, groomed and strapped him for another hour and kept his stable and gear spotless for another. This took him into the afternoon, by which time he was well into brooding about the Peter and Pip thing and not in a good state to be left unemployed, so he followed up the cramming job he had marked in the newspaper, and arranged to teach every afternoon from two to five, which saw him through to Dogwood's teatime and evening stables, after which his brain was too feeble to dwell overmuch on his misfortunes. After two or three months it became a way of life to which he became comparatively attached.

The teaching offered him a daily dose of civilization which kept his hand in, which he felt was fortunate for without it life at Mallow End was fairly brutalizing. Getting up was squalid for a start, for it was never worth lighting the fire for the minimal time it took to get dressed and washed and breakfasted, and there was often ice on the water-bucket or clamped over the dirty plates which were left in the washing-up bowl from the night before ...not an uplifting beginning to the day. Jonathan only started to get warm when he gave Dogwood his first dressing-over, or when he had trotted the first three miles of his morning marathon. After that it was sweat, mud and dung, in which he could no doubt have lived permanently like a pig save for the necessity of turning into a pedagogue sharp at two every afternoon. This entailed boiling up some water to wash in, which meant first doing the washing-up to free the bowl for ablutions, which meant making the place immediately less squalid and encouraged him to tidy the beds and sweep the fireplace, altogether a large step towards improving the living-standard. He would then rescue his clean jersey which he kept aired on Dogwood's back between his blanket and his day-rug, comb his hair and proceed on his motor-bike to Jasmine Cottage at Southavon where his pupil awaited him, a precocious thirteen-year-old by the name of Barnaby Potts who had something wrong with his spine and had to lie on his back for eighteen months. This in no way subdued his spirits, and Jonathan's teaching stint was no sinecure for the boy was sharp as a needle and looked forward eagerly to Jonathan's coming every day. Coming into the over-warm room and sitting down in an unaccustomedly comfortable chair was nearly Jonathan's undoing during the first few days but Mrs Potts, seeing him droop, got into the habit of supplying strong coffee which kept him in the necessary state of consciousness until five o'clock.

Fortunately Barnaby had a syllabus and books supplied from the school he had been attending which were the same Jonathan had once studied at Meddington, and the whole scene came back to him without any trouble, so that the job became a pleasant interlude in his day and a contact with the outside world, for which he actually got paid—quite well too, for Mrs Potts was pleased that she had found someone attractive to Barnaby, and not a retired elderly lady as she had feared, and upped her rate. Barnaby was enchanted with a tutor that trained a Grand National horse, but slightly disappointed he was not going to ride it.

'Why not?'

'Because I am training it for the person who *is* going to ride him—it's his life's ambition.'

'To win the Grand National?'

'No. To ride in it. To get round. Winning is a bit unlikely when you haven't got the experience.'

'Not impossible though.'

'Well, no, I suppose not.' Nothing was impossible in racing. 'It's a good horse. If we were terribly lucky, we might.'

'Have you ever ridden in a race?'

'Yes, quite a lot. I'm an amateur though. My friend's a professional. I ride in point-to-point, which counts as amateur racing.'

'They wouldn't let you ride in the Grand National?'

'Yes, if I applied for a permit. Amateurs can ride in professional races but professionals can't ride in amateur races.'

Which was the reason, eventually, that he got an invitation to visit the stable where Peter and Pip worked, because they were short of a jockey, the owner's son having broken his arm in a motor-bike accident.

'They must know someone around,' he said rather shortly, when Peter broached the subject.

'Well, I told them you were good,' Peter said. 'You could get a ride every Saturday if you wanted. I thought you'd be pleased.'

It was impossible to tell Peter how the invitation rankled. However hard he tried not to be, he was still intensely jealous of Peter's working with Pip and it helped a lot not to think about it, not to know. Now, to be invited into the set-up and spend a day witnessing how well Peter now got on with Pip was not going to help at all. For he did. It had been fairly inevitable, Peter being, after all, a handsome enough lad with a strong, humourous per-sonality and no hang-ups about wooing. Their relationship was enviably easy; they laughed a lot and teased, and put their arms round each other and kissed, not with passion

88

but with obvious affection. Jonathan supposed that if he was sensible he could join in and laugh and put his arm round Pip in the same friendly way, but the possibility brought him out in a cold sweat, and he knew that he was doomed to suffer. It did not help that she was invariably nice to him, always quick to include him in, never appeared to want to be alone with Peter. He loved her desperately, and was equally desperate not to let it show, which was why it helped to stay out of the picture.

'We told old Hargreaves you would ride for him on Saturday,' Pip said. 'You'll let us all down if you refuse. It's a good horse, nearly always starts favourite.'

'I'll do Dogwood on Saturday and you go with Pip,' Peter said.

Did he guess, Jonathan wondered? The lure was too much to resist.

'I'll drive you over,' Pip said. 'I'll call for you about twelve. You can lie in bed all morning.'

It was impossible to say no after that. He found he was looking forward to the day's racing with a ridiculous excitement. Another groom was to bring the horse to the race-course and all he had to do was drive to the course with Pip and ride it. No grafts at all, and Pip's company all day ... Peter brought him a cup of tea in bed and he lay there listening to Peter mucking out Dogwood in the hall. 'Just like old times,' Peter said, coming back for his riding boots. 'You'll find Hargreaves' old nag feels a bit different after Dogwood. Hope you're not set in your ways.'

After Peter had gone Jonathan got up and dressed in the best gear he possessed for looking like a jockey going to work, which included a tie and a shirt, the first he had worn since leaving school, and a pair of decent trousers with creases in them. After that he felt so strange he had to sit still to calm himself, and by the time Pip came he was in such a state of nervous tension that even she noticed and laughed and said, 'You look quite nervous!'

As she supposed it was about riding he did not argue—

89

better that than she should guess the real reason. He picked up his bag of gear and followed her out to her Mini. It was a bitterly cold day but a good riding day, the ground not too wet. There was already a nice fug in the car from the heater which actually worked, and Jonathan settled down beside Pip with a lovely sense of physical and mental well-being, unaccustomed for so long to being anything but a working groom and a hack tutor, and now about to swan into high society with Pip at his side and a decent horse to show off on. Pip was wearing a medley of fine tweed and cashmere and suede in the approved county tradition and looked quite ravishing to his starved eyes, her splendid green eyes accentuated with make-up and her cheeks and lips glossed mysteriously and delicately with something she did not bother to wear when she picked Peter up for work. She also smelt not of horses but of something out of a bottle which expanded expensively in the hot confines of the Mini to add to Jonathan's sense of giddy luxury.

'You might find you know some of the people,' she said encouragingly. 'We're not so far from where you used to ride, after all. I can remember Florestan running here—Peter said that horse belonged to your family.'

This was not at all what he wanted to hear. If his mother were to turn up ... the mounting sweat broke out underneath his shirt collar, which felt like a noose. He murmured something non-commital.

What else had that Bigmouth told her, he wondered?

'Mr Hargreaves remembered you riding that horse, Florestan,' Pip went on. 'You fell at the last jump and remounted, or something. He said it was very impressive.'

'Christ! He saw that? Peter won that race.' He had wanted to kill him. 'What's he like, this Hargreaves bloke? I might know him.'

'Elderly. Red face, drinks a lot. Won't care if you don't win, so don't worry. He just likes the scene, talking and boozing.'

'Do you ever ride? In races, I mean?'

'No. Daddy won't let me.'

Daddy wouldn't, Jonathan supposed. Mummy made him, and was wicked if he didn't get it right. How lovely to ride for the inebriated Mr Hargreaves who didn't care! Jonathan felt his heart lifting, the smell of Pip's scent intoxicating.

'You smell gorgeous!'

She laughed.

'Better than dung! It's Diorissima. You like it?'

She glanced sideways at him in what he would have thought was quite a come-on way, if he hadn't seen her with Peter.

'Mmm. Terribly civilized.'

'Well, you look pretty civilized today.'

'Makes a change, have to impress the guv'nor....' He felt himself flushing slightly. Her too, if she but knew it.

Pip came to a crossing, stopped, changed gear, waited for a tractor.

'Is Peter serious about the Grand National? I'm never quite sure. If you ask him, he makes jokes about it.'

Jonathan was surprised. 'He's deadly serious.'

'It's quite an undertaking—the National—'

'That's the point, isn't it? He's got the chance, with Dogwood. He's given everything else up to take it.'

'Will you go up to Aintree too?'

'Yes. I'm the lad, I think. The worker. Peter's the star-turn.'

'Can I come with you? I'd love to.'

'I should think so. Jockey's girl-friends aren't supposed to enjoy the National though,' he remembered, having read about it. 'You put your hands over your face and watch through little cracks between your fingers.'

She laughed.

'It's the horses I worry about.'

He thought that was rather a good sign, that she didn't care if Peter fell off and broke his neck. The thought of anything happening to Dogwood gave him a nasty qualm;

91

he was pretty devoted to the old brute, he realized, spending nearly all day in his company, and knew him better than anybody, Peter included. It was a horse's 'lad' that suffered in the jumping game if a horse was hurt, for the jockey never knew his mounts like the lad knew his particular horse. The jockey had often never set eyes on his horse before, just as he had never set eyes on—

'What's this horse I'm to ride this afternoon?'

'Black Cherry.'

'Has it got any nasty habits I should know about?'

'No. He jumps well, stays well. Ought to win, really.'

This did not cheer Jonathan up particularly. Better to do well on a horse nothing is expected of, than ride the favourite and not win. He lacked the killer instinct; rode races because he enjoyed it, not, if the truth were known, to win at all costs. Peter was the true competitor, although he had always hidden the fact fairly successfully under a flippant exterior. Peter, under starter's orders, was a different man.

Fortunately there did not seem to be any old friends of the family on the race-course, which allayed his major fears, and his introduction to Hargreaves confirmed his reputation as a harmless old buffer unlikely to tear his jockey off a strip if he failed to win.

'Jolly glad you can ride for me, dear boy. I just hope the old horse will give you a nice run round.'

Jonathan went off to change for the second race, the Adjacent Hunts, where he found he knew quite a few of his fellow jockeys, including....

'My God, Jonathan darling!'

Standing by the scales waiting to weigh out he was all but knocked down by the embraces of his ex-girl-friend, the one time Melissa Jones. Down on the card as Mrs C. Howarth, she had not registered with him as an acquaintance.

'How absolutely lovely to see you! I can't think of anybody else I would rather have in the same race with me, darling Jonathan!'

She was just as delicious as always, all curves and curls and exuberance; too old for him, unfortunately, hence her marrying the undeserving Clive Howarth. 'He's my owner now, Jonathan. He buys me horses to win on, money no object. Who are you riding today?'

'Something called Black Cherry.'

'Really?' He was glad to see she looked impressed. 'Well, that's one I have to beat. Dear Jonathan, I have missed you! Between you and me, secretly, you are a lot nicer than Clive, but then—' She laughed, shrugged. Even in riding gear she smelled every bit as good as Pip.

'Diorissima?' He sniffed expertly.

'Yes, Diorissima on the way out. Sweat and blood coming back in. I thought you were a drop-out, Jonathan? Run away, your mother told me. I was ever so pleased.'

'Yes, and if you see her, for God's sake not a word. You do understand, don't you?'

'Knowing her, yes, darling. Mum's the word.'

They weighed out, Jonathan feeling the nervous excitement beginning to get hold of him, whether because of Melissa or Black Cherry he did not know. When they went out into the paddock Melissa huddled up close to him, her arm round his waist, chattering happily, and he had to disentangle in front of Pip's interested gaze, and take his leave for the time being, to confront his mount and his mount's owner.

'Friend of yours, eh, the delectable Mrs Clive Howarth?' old Hargreaves boomed cheerfully.

Jonathan, burning hot in spite of the bitter wind, said lamely, 'A friend of my family's,' caught Pip's cynical eye and blushed. Pip, changed temporarily into a working anorak and gumboots, was holding Black Cherry for him and another groom was stripping off the horse's rugs. It was a lean, angular dark bay, grinding its bit in anticipation. The groom gave Jonathan a leg-up. After Dogwood, Black Cherry felt like a towel-rail. Groping for his stirrups, Jonathan felt the usual panics rising at what he was taking on, and was glad when Pip led the horse on round the paddock so that he did not have to make polite chat any more but start to feel himself into what he was doing. It was a serious business, after all, riding in a race; pre-race nerves were an inevitable part of it. He spared a thought for Peter when it came Grand National time—the imagination boggled. The comparison calmed him. Pip looked up at him and he grinned. Perhaps she was thinking the same.

'Okay?'

He nodded. She unclipped the leading-rein.

'Good luck then. Look after yourself.'

Black Cherry lobbed straight into a bold canter to go down to the start and Jonathan immediately started to enjoy himself. As always, the experience confirmed that there was absolutely nothing in life to compare with riding towards a big fence at full gallop on a good horse in company with a dozen others; everything else was forgotten. Black Cherry felt good, and gave him a superlative ride, so that three-quarters of the way through the race he was up alongside the delectable Melissa with every indication of having far more in hand than she had and with only two fast-tiring horses in front of him. He glanced across at her and grinned again. She was splattered with mud and the Diorissima was, as she had predicted, scattered to the cold winds but she had a man's determination on her face; it was not only Mr Howarth's money he had to beat but Mrs Howarth's professionalism. Black Cherry held her fairly comfortably but Jonathan knew from hard experience there were no foregone conclusions until the winning post was past. As if to prove it, at the second last fence the tired horse in front of him ran out and in so doing crossed Black Cherry's path two strides before take-off, which resulted in considerable mayhem. Jonathan sailed over the fence quite separately from his horse, although they landed together on their backs. Melissa jumped them both, as well as the fence, and went on to win, and Jonathan walked back alone, covered in mud and aching in several places, not least in his self-esteem.

'I say, hard cheese, old man,' said Hargreaves happily. 'Have a nip, do you good.' He handed him a whisky flask. 'You had it in the bag, I'd say—except for the young lady, perhaps. Next Saturday, eh? Get your own back. Well done, old chap.'

Jonathan was slightly bemused at this reception, comparing it with what he would have got from his mother under the circumstances, and went into the changing-room feeling undamaged in spirit, if not entirely in body. It had been good, after all, until the curtains. He ached all over and longed for a hot bath but life wasn't offering hot baths at that point; he changed and gathered his kit together and went out to find Pip again. She looked pleased to see him, might have been said to be waiting for him, Jonathan thought optimistically. He felt a bit of a fool, not having impressed her in the way he had hoped to, riding nonchalantly into the winner's enclosure to the plaudits of the crowd.

'Bad luck! Poor old you! Are you all right?'

'Yes, no damage, only to the ego.'

'Oh, it wasn't your fault. You were going beautifully. Such a shame! Put your bag away in my car and we'll go and have a drink.'

They watched the rest of the races and he was introduced to a great many people and found his head aching by the end of the afternoon, not from his fall but in the general confusion of being in such a crowd after his weeks of solitary living. He was not sorry when Pip headed for the car-park at last; after all, being alone with her was almost as good as riding the race. The intimacy of the little car, knee to knee, was right up his street. With luck there would be a few more Saturdays like this.

'Do you want to come home and have a meal? I'm sure my mother wouldn't mind.'

He said the right, polite thing, trying to hide his elation. Had she ever asked Peter to a meal? Peter had never said so, although he had been late in a few times, without any specific reason why. Jonathan had never thought to ask.

It was astonishing how lovely civilization was after all these weeks: things like carpets and curtains and softly-shaded lights, the news on the television and sitting at a proper table with everything in dishes. Pip's parents seemed to have unfrozen since first impressions, and were welcoming and approving. They were curious about why he and Peter were doing what they were, but too polite to ask directly. Jonathan wasn't sure how much Peter had told Pip; he was as non-commital as possible, trying to suggest that he had left school and was filling in time before he decided what to do for a career. There was absolutely no call for them to know about Iris, especially Pip. Pip had the most extraordinary effect on him. He could not take his eyes off her in her home setting, her cashmere covered with an apron while she helped dish up a joint of pork in the kitchen and mashed the apple sauce smooth, saying very little but catching his eye and smiling occasionally as he made suitable conversation with her father. Her mother was plump and unassuming, and not disposed to join in the conversation unless directly appealed to. Slightly downtrodden, Jonathan judged, taking the path of least resistance; her husband, although now being relatively amiable, could revert to his prison-warder stance at the drop of a hat in Jonathan's opinion. Women and children definitely under father's thumb.

When it was time for him to go Pip said she would drive him back. He made a token resistance: 'Really, I can walk. It's no distance.'

'It's raining,' Pip said.

They went out to the Mini and drove in silence down the farm road and into the cutting through the woods, the car's lights slicing a bright swathe ahead. Jonathan knew that this was the moment for him to say all the clever, smoothie things that a practised suitor would come up with at such a moment, but his mouth was dry and he could not think of a word to say. Pip pulled up on the gravel outside Dogwood's front door. Jonathan sat like a zombie.

'It's been a nice day,' Pip said.

'Yes. Thank you.' He blundered for the door-latch, his heart thudding. He had managed with other girls, he thought furiously, who didn't matter, but when it *mattered*—

'We'll do it again,' she said.

'Yes.'

He sat there, the door open, the rain driving in, turned to stone. He looked at her and she smiled. His heart came up into his mouth.

'Pip, I—'

He half-turned, seeing her feelings—or so he thought—and at that moment a long shaft of light fell across them as the front door opened under the portico and Peter's silhouette stood at the top of the steps.

'Hi! Ride any winners?'

Peter ambled out into the rain, openly pleased to see them. 'I'm lonely,' he said. 'Coming in?' He went to Pip's side of the car, opened the door and kissed her amiably on the ear. 'Is he as good as I said?'

'Better,' Pip said, and laughed.

'Come in for a bit.'

'No. Dad'll be cross. You know what he's like.'

Jonathan got out into the rain. His ardour was drenched. He was stone-cold, sick. The Mini turned round and Pip waved to them, smiling, and he went in through the front door with Peter. What had she meant, 'better'?

'How was it?' Peter asked.

Jonathan wanted to say, ruined, blasted, decimated....
'We fell at the second last. Okay till then. Horse in front ran across us.'

'Bad luck. Is he giving you another ride?'

'Next Saturday, he said.'

'Fine. He must have thought you were okay then.' Peter bolted the door securely from Dogwood's curious lips and they went through into the living-quarters. 'I had a letter from my brother,' Peter said. 'He says he's got Dogwood down to run at Ascot on Wednesday—this Wednesday ...I rang him and he said he'd see us there. It's a three and a half mile chase, quite stiff opposition—not that we're expected to win. Just give him a reminder what a race-course looks like.'

'Ascot?'

'We'll have to set off early. It's quite a way.'

'You're the jockey, I take it?'

'Of course. We'll see if Pip'll come too, shall we? Make it a bit of a jaunt.'

'Mmm. Fine.'

Ascot was a bit different from a country point-to-point; this was serious. Peter had the lead part this time, and he would be relegated to the role of lad. Would Pip be able to come?

Peter said, 'We'll take Dogwood over to Hargreaves' tomorrow and give him a school, so he remembers what a jump looks like. He's been leading rather a sheltered life lately.'

They drove him over in the hearse, Pip sitting between them in the front. It was spitting with rain, grey clouds rolling in from the sea. Life was getting real, life was getting earnest, Jonathan was thinking: he had not yet thought seriously that the Grand National was going to happen, but now ... it was only a couple of months away and Ascot, even Ascot, was definitely the real thing. None of your amateur fun-day out-in-the-country, but hard-bitten professional racing, up against the best. Was Dogwood the best?

Getting him out of the trailer, stripping off his rugs in the neat Hargreaves yard, Jonathan saw him against an unfamiliar background, as race-goers would appraise him in the paddock, and felt an instinctive lurch of pride for his charge. He looked as fit as a horse could possibly look, lean and muscled and shining, his bold gaze taking in his new surroundings, big ears pricked, nostrils quivering. He was an intelligent horse and looked it. Jonathan felt a stupid tremor of sentiment disturbing his equanimity as he thought of the old boy going to Aintree.

'He's jumped it before,' Peter had already told him. 'He was fourth in the Foxhunters.'

The Foxhunters was a race run over the Grand National course (but only one circuit as opposed to two for the National). He had already proved he could cope with Aintree, but he was twelve now, about as old as a horse had any hope, and his legs, strained by hard racing, were no longer guaranteed to hold him up like a youngster's.

'What happens to chasers like this when their racing days are over?' Pip asked, as if struck by the same thoughts. 'What will you do with him next year?'

'I suppose he'll go back to my brother's,' Peter said.

'I thought you said they were thinking of putting him down,' Jonathan said belligerently. He had taken it for granted earlier, but the thought roused him now.

'Even if he goes back, he can't race for much longer, surely?' Pip said.

'No. Well, you retire 'em. Find 'em a nice home hunting or hacking.'

'What, Dogwood?' Jonathan was sceptical, knowing Dogwood's lethal habits. Dogwood was no lady's hunter, not even a strong man's, if he wanted a safe and enjoyable day. It was difficult to find a suitable job for a retired racehorse such as Dogwood Jonathan knew only too well, and he realized now, thinking about it, that he was going to care very much what happened to Dogwood after the National. It was a disturbing thought, to add to all the other disturbing thoughts as to what was going to happen after the National. In a strange way to all three of them, Peter himself and the horse, after the National was a great blank. '*Christ*! he thought, with a sudden shiver, what were they thinking of?

Peter tightened Dogwood's girths and Jonathan gave

him a leg-up. Although Jonathan had no wish at all to ride Dogwood in the National he felt a slight resentment at seeing Peter sitting up there on 'his' horse. Doing a horse every day certainly inspired a sense of proprietorship.

They went out into the fields. The schooling jumps were set up beside a small strip of woodland, two of them built into existing hedgerow and two in the open. Peter rode away to give Dogwood a warm-up and Jonathan and Pip walked slowly up the hill to the best view-point. Jonathan was once more acutely aware that he was alone with Pip, but sensed that her attention was on Peter.

To prove it, she said, 'Riding these jumps is one thing. Those Aintree fences are another altogether. I'm glad it's not me.'

Jonathan would once have agreed without hesitation on the last utterance, but his instinct now veered towards envy because of his strong sense of kinship with Dogwood. If Dogwood was to face the ultimate test, Dogwood would like him along, Jonathan felt sure. As much as a horse took to anyone, Jonathan knew that Dogwood had taken to him. But Dogwood was an old stager compared with himself. And watching Peter, Jonathan knew that Peter by comparison with himself was an old stager too. He had probably put in more horse-hours in his lifetime than many an older jockey and it showed in the way he sat, the way Dogwood settled for him and accepted him immediately, knowing sympathy when he felt it.

Watching, Pip said, 'He is a lovely rider. He must have a great future, if he gets the breaks—lucky ones, I mean, not fractures.'

It was nice to know somebody had a future, Jonathan thought. That left him and Dogwood.

He had never seen Dogwood jump before and was impressed by the boldness of his take-off, the power in his hocks. Peter went round a couple of times, and the horse was impeccable.

'No point doing any more,' Peter remarked, coming

back to his two spectators. 'He doesn't need it.'

'He's got a powerful jump.'

'Yes, he's always like that. Probably take too much out of him at Aintree, jumping like that. He likes to clear them by too much, the silly old fool.'

'Better than trying to brush through them, surely? That'll put you in the cart up there.'

'Yes, but he doesn't have to be such a show-off. He doesn't know about economical jumping, just as much as you need and no more. You'd have thought he'd have realized by now.'

'He enjoys it, by the look of him.'

'He feels like it. He feels super. He's a great fellow.'

Peter leant forward and pulled Dogwood's ears affectionately.

'Suppose he wins?' Pip enquired.

'Suppose,' Peter said, poker-faced.

'How much do you win?'

'My brother wins it. Something like sixty thousand pounds.'

'The jockey gets ten per cent. And the lad gets four,' Pip said. 'We'll all go out to dinner.'

'We're not entering to win,' Peter said.

'Suppose you can't help it? You can't not have thought about winning *at all*?'

'It's so remotely possible, to *win*—a jockey's first ride.'

Pip looked up at him sternly. 'I defy you—I absolutely defy you—to admit that you haven't just once or twice thought about winning—pictured yourself being led in between the police horses and everybody going mad—?'

Peter grinned. 'Like you dream sometimes about— what?—marrying the Prince of Wales and being Queen of England?—too late now, but you know what I mean.'

'Racing's full of fairy stories. That's what keeps 'em all going.'

'It needs to be. It's full of disasters too.'

'You won't be a disaster, Peter darling! It's going to be

101

terribly exciting!'

'Let's get there first, think about it then. Anything can happen between now and April.

It happened the very next day.

Peter rang up his brother in a panic.

'Dogwood can't run on Wednesday. We've had a bit of an accident down here.'

'He's injured? What happened?'

When Peter told him, Geoff wouldn't believe it.

'A chandelier fell on him? Are you out of your mind?'

'No, for Christ's sake, it's the truth. He's all cut about, nothing deep, but a bit of a mess.'

Geoff was silent for some time, trying to assimilate this unlikely story. Then he said, 'Where was he at the time?'

'In his stable.'

Another long pause. 'I don't use chandeliers myself,' he said, and rang off.

Neither Peter nor Jonathan were in when it happened. Jonathan came back from his teaching stint and found Dogwood standing indignantly by the front door, his eyes out on stalks and his bedding covered with debris of not only the the chandelier but a goodly proportion of the ceiling as well. If the horse had been immediately underneath it the boys reckoned he would have been killed. As it was he seemed to have been somewhere within the firing range, for he had a deep cut on his neck and another, the most serious as far as his career was concerned, on a front fetlock. Until that was healed there was no question of his moving out of a walk.

'Ten days about,' Peter said gloomily when he came home and surveyed the battlefield. 'Bloody hell!'

Jonathan had already treated the cut with stuff out of Peter's vet's kit, and bandaged it after Peter had assessed the damage. They tied the horse up and started clearing up the mess, trundling the debris into the adjoining drawing-room in the wheelbarrow and clearing all the straw out to make sure there was no broken glass lurking for their ace-horse to tread on. It took them all the evening. Dogwood was shocked and kept breaking out in a sweat; the draught roared through the hole in the ceiling and the landing windows rattled in their sockets. The February wind was cold as charity, and the boys' spirits were to match. They stoked up their fireplace and brewed tea and sat staring into the flames at midnight, as shaken by Dogwood at how fragile were their ambitions, how thorny their path and foggy their future.

'It's all crazy really,' Peter said.

Jonathan thought of Iris and felt deeply depressed. She had sheered him off from his comfortable, planned future and some time soon—after the Grand National—he was going to have to decide something. Now he realized for the first time there might not even be a Grand National. . . .

Peter's face in the firelight was bleak.

'It's crazy what I'm doing, wasting all this time just for a chance to ride round Aintree. I should be getting the rides now, plugging away at it. I think I'll pack in Hargreaves next week and see if I can get some rides between now and April. After all, I'm not going to be fit enough if I don't.'

'You ride all day, don't you?'

'You know as well as I do you only get fit enough to ride races by riding races.'

'Mmm.' It was a fact.

'Moneywise, we can get by, I should think,' Peter said. 'After all, if I get some rides I'll get paid for them. And if I don't, at the worst, I should think we could scrape by as far as April.'

It was true that their living costs were minimal, a good deal less than Dogwood's.

Peter departed the following week for his brother's, taking the hearse because its owner was now recovered and wanted it back. He hitch-hiked back a few days later and said he had been offered a ride at Fakenham on Friday and at Huntingdon the following Tuesday. He was jubilant.

'How are you going to get there?' Jonathan asked.

'I thought you'd lend me your motor-bike.'

'How am I going to get to work in the afternoon?'

Peter considered. 'Pip's got a bike,' he suggested.

Jonathan, even as he dismissed the idea with scornful laugh, knew it was going to happen, and so it did.

Peter was fourth in a selling race at Fakenham and fell at Huntingdon.

'But the trainer thought I rode okay and has booked me for another at Plumpton on Tuesday.'

Jonathan was booked to ride every Saturday for Hargreaves. Each time Peter came too and loused up Jonathan's chances with Pip. Time started to slip by and even if Jonathan got nowhere with Pip he was getting somewhere with Dogwood, who was pronounced fit to run and entered in a race at Folkestone some three weeks before the Grand National.

'God, he could have done with two races ... that bloody chandelier!'

Peter took him out and discovered that he could canter effortlessly for miles without showing the slightest sign of sweat or weariness, and long walks along the beach in the sea had cleared up his fetlock injury more successfully than they had dared hope.

'You're a pretty good trainer, Meredith, I'll say that for you. Perhaps that's what you should do for a living, now your daddy won't have you in his tower block.'

Training was hard and cold and worrying. His father's work was hard and worrying but centrally-heated—Jonathan was in no fit state to take decisions.

'How are we going to get to Folkestone? As trainer, am I supposed to have arranged that?'

'I thought we might borrow the Hargreaves horse-box. I'll ask him—he can only say no.'

Hargreaves said yes. The horse-box was vast and

required an HGV certificate to drive it.

'I bet you haven't got one?' Jonathan challenged Peter.

'Wrong again. I have.'

'It'll take about a hundred gallons of diesel to get there and back.'

'Hmm. You exaggerate, but yes, expensive. But dear Weatherbys send me cheques these days, remember. I will pay, do not worry.'

'I hope dear Weatherby's won't notice that we're breaking a few rules, like our horse not actually being trained by the man who says he's the trainer, and not living where he's supposed to be living.'

'With luck by the time they notice we shall have done what we want. Geoff said he'd come to Folkestone and do the necessary. He said he'll get you and Pip a pass—that means yer photos in glorious technicolour. You'll need them for Aintree anyway.'

'Good.' Perhaps they could go and get their photos taken together, Jonathan thought. They could sit in a little dark booth together....

'I've got one,' Pip said. 'I can take it off my student card. It'll do, won't it?'

'Fine. What were you a student of, as a matter of interest?'

'Psychology. I didn't like it.'

'I'm not surprised.'

Perhaps she knew what he was thinking with a year of psychology behind her? God help him. Perhaps while Peter was riding she would hold his hand in the stands? No, while Peter was riding he would be in no fit state to think of sex. Already the thought of seeing Dogwood on the race-course made him sweat. The days were flying past. Dogwood was bursting out of his skin with health and vigour. Roll on, Aintree, Jonathan thought. Anything could happen.

Chapter 6

The day Dogwood ran at Folkestone was cold, wet and windy. Although Pip was of the party, Jonathan had no thoughts beyond the welfare of Dogwood as he led him round the paddock before the race. The horse was fit to jump out of his skin and even at a walk pulled so hard that Jonathan was sweating and steaming before he had gone four circuits. Dogwood ground his teeth on his bit making a noise like rocks rolling down a precipice and watched the crowd around the paddock with a malicious eye. Peter was afraid that he might stage an exhibition of what he called 'the aversions' but so far he had not done anything out of place. Fortunately Geoff had arrived with a horse for another race, and so had taken on the trainer's duties; he had been impressed with Dogwood's condition and congratulated them—which is more than could be said for his own; he was haggard and pale. He was standing in the centre of the paddock talking to another trainer, trilby tipped against the rain. The cold air smelled of the sea and the afternoon was one for crumpets by the fire, to Jonathan's way of thinking. His hands were raw and Dogwood was fast giving him blisters. He was infinitely relieved when the jockeys came out and the bell rang for the horses to be mounted.

Peter came up with Geoff, grinning happily. His colours were a sickening mixture of orange, green and purple which Jonathan could see he would have no difficulty in keeping an eye on even in the prevailing murk; they did little for his complexion which was somewhat jaundiced by the pills he had been taking to get his weight down to the ten stone seven Dogwood had been allocated. Jonathan felt much as Peter looked, without the pills.

Dogwood did not want to stand still and Peter was legged up with a rush and Jonathan dragged half the length of the paddock before their combined strength got him back to a dignified pace again. Geoff ran behind gathering up the rugs, and then they were out and heading for the course between the streams of blue-faced punters making for the stands. Peter was pulling up the girths.

'Christ, wait until it's Aintree!' he said.

'Don't get hurt, for God's sake,' Jonathan said, but he was thinking of Dogwood. He unclipped the leading-rein. 'Okay?'

He let go and Dogwood bounded up into the rain and hurtled down past the stands. Watching, Jonathan saw Peter gather him together, steady him, saw his great raking stride lob him down across the squelchy grass, felt his stomach churn with apprehension.

He turned away to go up into the stands, and found Pip standing beside him.

'I'm nervous,' she said.

'That makes two of us.'

Jonathan took her arm without thinking and guided her towards the nearest stand. They climbed up the steps, high to get a good view, and the wind and the rain blew in. The bookies were shouting the odds below them, their big umbrellas heaving uneasily. Pip did not say anything, pulling the collar of her furlined coat up round her ears, watching the distant horses through her binoculars. It was different from point-to-points, Jonathan was thinking; the whole thing was for real. Until now it had just been a game of Peter's, a useful way of opting out, but now he saw that they were part of a business, a whole way of life in which people depended for a living on the likes of him and Dogwood. He felt chastened and inadequate, and terribly excited, and had to make a conscious effort not to let any of it show.

The start was away in the murk on the far side of the

course and even the binoculars, Pip reported, did not reveal anything but a blur, but shortly the loud-speaker came to life with the familiar, 'They're under starter's orders,' followed almost immediately by 'They're off!'

There were ten runners and three and a quarter miles to go, and the pace in the soggy conditions was very moderate. As they came up to the water-jump opposite the stands for the first time Dogwood was the last horse, but loping along very easily. He jumped the water as if launching off the nearby cliffs to reach France and lobbed away round the bend throwing up wet clods behind him. There were two full circuits still to go, the finish being alongside the water-jump. Peter was sitting still not bothering and Jonathan decided not to bother too, seeing how Dogwood jumped. It might not be economical but it was definitely confidence-boosting. But in spite of his resolution he found he was grinding his fingers together and holding his breath at every jump . . .

'There's a faller at the open ditch!' said the commentator. 'It's Dogwood—no, it's Lady Limborne! Lady Limborne a faller there!'

Jonathan let out a groan. He had never guessed it would be so awful. The silly, bloody horse . . . don't get hurt, Dogwood! Peter, you idiot, look after him! He tried to pull himself together, ashamed of his neurotics. They were coming into the home straight again, with another circuit to go, and Dogwood was still at the back, with one horse behind him now, and pinging the jumps as if they were all twice as big. His stride was still easy and he pricked his ears momentarily towards the buzzing of spectators, and as he went away round the bend he went past the horse in front and started improving on the others.

'He's going a treat!' Pip murmured. 'Oh, Peter! He's fantastic!'

Jonathan could not speak, squinting into the half-darkness of the terrible weather, seeing the blur of Peter's unhappy colours going into the open ditch only six lengths

behind the leaders. Dogwood was steadily making up
ground, yet Jonathan knew the intention was not to win,
but just to have a sensible race, a practice for next month.
The ground was terrible and all the horses floundering as
they came round the long bend at the far end of the course
towards the home straight. Dogwood had jumped without
putting a foot wrong. They were heading straight into the
rain and two of the leaders packed it in, dropping back
abruptly. Pip started to dance about.

'He's third! *Third!* Oh, don't fall, Dogwood! Keep
going, Dogwood!'

Jonathan felt sick as they came to the last. The two
leading horses were fighting a duel of their own, and
Dogwood was about three lengths behind, going fairly
easily. All three horses jumped well, but Dogwood made a
full length on the other two. He pecked a fraction on
landing, but Peter sat still and held him together. The
crowd started to yell.

'He could win! He could win! Dogwood!' Pip screamed.

But Peter was not riding a hard race, not with the
National so close. He did not pick up his whip, but rode
Dogwood out strongly enough to please the stewards: the
two leaders fought a merciless battle, whips flailing, all the
way to the line and finished with only a neck between
them, with Dogwood a perky third, four lengths back.

Pip flung her arms round Jonathan.

'He was splendid! Good old Dogwood! Aren't you
pleased?'

Jonathan suddenly was, very much so, all his hard work
as trainer vindicated. The old horse was fresher than
nearly all his rivals and had run with every indication of
enthusiasm. He took his opportunity, confidence flooding
him. He kissed Pip on the lips, reckless and happy. She was
cold and rain-splashed and the experience was stunning.
She did not pull away but kissed him back with happy
enthusiasm. For Dogwood's victory? It could not be called
a passionate kiss, but Jonathan thought there was more to

it than pure joy. It gave him the trembles, wondering, but it was no moment to linger, to push his luck. She was laughing, moving away. He had to laugh too, cover up what he felt, pretend it didn't matter. They had to run, pushing their way down the steps, to lead Dogwood in. He wanted to shout at her, 'I do love you, Pip! I do love you!' but of course he did nothing of the sort. She was running as fast as he was, to greet Peter. One did not kiss jockeys on the way to the winning enclosure, but did she want to? Jonathan could not make it out. He half wanted to himself, so pleased that they had done so well after all the months of hard grind—such emotion could hardly be muddled with love. Peter was grinning, his face half white where the goggles had been, half black with mud.

'Didn't put a foot wrong! It was a fantastic ride!'

They led him in through the crowd and Geoff came to meet them. Peter unsaddled and went to weigh in and then Jonathan was leading Dogwood back to the stables. Pip came with him. It was all work now, and nothing was said about the kiss, but Jonathan could not stop thinking about it. Pip went to get hot water to wash Dogwood down, and Jonathan watched her, tough and competent. He loved her for all the right reasons; she was the sort one needed to live with.

'Idiot! Fool.' he said to himself, pretending he meant Dogwood, who would not stand still as Jonathan attempted to undo the bandages on his forelegs. He did not want to be committed, but he was in earnest about Pip. It was hopeless. Everything was stupid. Yet he felt amazingly, fantastically happy.

She came back and they washed the old horse down, talking rubbish to him, and joking, towelling him off. They both got soaked themselves, and all the mud off Dogwood seemed to finish up on them. They wound on his big fat travelling bandages and rugged him up, by which time Peter came back with Geoff and they all went to the lads' cafe for a cup of tea. The rain beat on the window and the fug got nicely into their bones and the talk was all of doing well, a cautious optimism, great satisfaction with the day's work.

'If I'd really ridden him out, I could have beaten those two,' Peter said. 'But it would have done him no good.'

'No. You did the right thing,' Geoff said. 'He hasn't run as well as that for a long time.'

'It's Jonathan's influence, all those man-hours he's put in straightening out his kinks.'

'Yeah, well, he always needed understanding. I only hope his legs'll hold out for the big race. See how he is tomorrow.'

'You coming to Aintree?' Peter asked his brother.

'Yes, of course.'

They loaded Dogwood into the big Hargreaves' box and Peter climbed up into the driving-seat. He had got himself booked for two more races before Aintree, which pleased him.

'My career is taking off,' he said.

'More than you can say for mine,' Jonathan said.

'No. Well ... you never wanted Oxford, did you?'

Pip was sitting between them. Jonathan could feel her thigh against his own, and did not want anything changed, career or no career. He was working out when he could wangle another chance to kiss Pip. If Peter won the National that would be worth any amount of passionate embracing ... he was grinning to himself, looking forward to the drama ahead. The lights glittered on the road ahead, striking sparks from the cats-eyes; the big lorry thundered northwards, full of dreams. Only Dogwood was immune, munching his haynet in the back, easing his old legs at intervals in the deep straw.

In the morning the old legs were filled and the horse moved stiffly. Peter said, 'If they'll just last out the big one...'

'You wouldn't ride him if—' Jonathan's voice was indignant.

'No, twit. But he's been dicey for years. Half the chasers running are in the same state. And I'm not going to ride him hard, I promise you. I just don't want to miss the chance, that's all.'

They rested him two days, just taking him out for a graze on the front lawn, and then he was back to himself, the stiffness gone. The legs were clean, the optimism bounding. Jonathan rode him out again, and was troubled by what was going to happen afterwards, not to himself, but to Dogwood. There wasn't a great future for broken-down chasers. They did not retire easily, used to a hard life. He rode him down the deep sandy ways towards the sea, across the shingly fore-shores and for miles along the beach and back through the forest. It had become a ritual now, and as the days were counted off towards the big race Jonathan felt a deep regret rising up at the coming demise of a great partnership. It was illogical, for it was never intended to become the routine of a lifetime, but it marked an interval in Jonathan's life which he could see now was only temporary; Dogwood was destined to mark a milestone; his life was going to divide neatly into before and after Dogwood.

If he ever gave Iris a thought, it was only for the comparative stage of her pregnancy come Grand National time; she would be eight months. One month more and all would be resolved. The routine at Ravenshall would be decided and he would be made a stranger there, or not, as the case might be. He found he could accept it now, even welcome it, for the whole business had given him independence from his overbearing family. He was his own man, for better or for worse. He had come to terms with it and now regretted nothing. A new confidence was his reward and he stopped feeling guilty and hard-done-by and began to look forward not only to the big race, but to what might happen afterwards.

On the Saturday before the National Peter went to Newbury to ride in a novice hurdle race. He took Jonathan's motor-bike and drove over the evening before and stayed the night with his brother. The Saturday was foggy but the racing was not cancelled; Jonathan heard the news on his transistor. But by late evening Peter had not returned and Jonathan began to get worried. It might, he thought, be due to the weather. On the other hand, the racing game being as it was, it might be due to ... perish the thought! Jonathan could not bear to dwell on it, but became progressively more fidgety as the evening progressed. Peter could not phone him, and Jonathan did not fancy venturing to the nearest phone-box to phone Geoff without any transport. It was over a mile to get out of the park, let alone find a phone-box. He listened to his transistor and read some back numbers of 'Horse and Hound' which Pip had brought them, but nothing seemed of interest. By eleven o'clock he was standing at the window, nose pressed to the glass to survey the inky darkness outside, supposing it was time to go to bed, but not feeling anything like falling asleep. As he watched a light swooped suddenly on the trees across the lawn, beaming out of the driveway through the woods, and headlights came towards the house. It was a car, not a motor-bike. He went out through Dogwood's quarters and opened the front door, taking the torch.

'What is it?'

It was Pip, scrambling out of her Mini.

'It's Peter—he rang—I had to come and tell you—'

Jonathan could see that she was upset, and knew that his worst fears were to be confirmed.

'He had a fall?'

'Yes. His collar-bone's gone. Nothing terrible but—enough—he—he was almost crying.'

It was like the chandelier falling all over again, the shock and disappointment almost too much to take. Jonathan could not trust himself to say anything unless he too burst into tears—all that work! Peter's ride down the drain ... a week was too short to mend in, and nothing could be done about it. It was the perennial risk the job entailed, not just to get hurt, but to get sidelined for the big chance. And how Peter had planned and looked forward to it! He had shaped his whole life towards that one ride for the last six months.

'You'd better come in,' Jonathan said numbly.

He shoved Dogwood out of the way, slapping the iron-hard muscle of his neck. Dogwood knuckered, pushing at him affectionately, and a lump of choking disappointment came up into Jonathan's throat. He groped for the door-handle to his own quarters, and ushered Pip towards the dishevelled hearth. The fire had fallen low and he threw a log on, and stood watching the fresh flame lick up over the pine bark. The sweet resinous smell crept up into his nostrils.

'Poor Peter!'

It was worse for Peter, however bad he himself might feel. And he felt bad enough.

Pip stood beside him, looking at the flames. She shivered. Jonathan put his arm around her shoulders, with no thought beyond a mutual comfort.

'Did he say—no, it's a bit soon, I suppose...' It meant Dogwood running with another jockey. That would be for Geoff to decide.

'He said you would have to ride him.'

Jonathan laughed. 'I can't. I haven't got a permit.'

'Peter said there's time for you to get one. You've got the qualifications.'

Jonathan dropped his arm abruptly, the suggestion shaking him.

Pip went on, 'He said could I come up and collect him because he can't ride the motor-bike, and if you come you can fill in the forms, which Geoff has got, Geoff can sign them and you can go straight to London on Monday and call in at the Jockey Club and collect a permit.'

'You're joking?'

'No. I'm only saying what he said on the phone. He sounded very much in earnest to me.'

'Well, I can see that Dogwood ought to run, but if Peter can't ride him I would have thought we could find an experienced jockey to take him on.'

'Why? The whole point of entering him was to give Peter the ride. If he can't do it now, surely you don't want to give up the opportunity?'

Jonathan looked at Pip dubiously, to see if she was serious, or teasing. But no, she looked determined and anxious. He saw at once that he was cornered, and could scarcely credit what was happening: she, misguided girl, thought he was of the same calibre as Peter, eager as hell to risk his neck. If he backed out she would consider him (quite rightly) chicken. To prevaricate, he said, 'Did you agree to drive over to Berkshire to pick him up?'

'Yes. It's Sunday so I haven't got to go to work. You will come too?'

'I'll have to ride Dogwood first.'

'Yes, well, we'll go after that. I can get someone to feed him in the evening, if we're late back.'

Jonathan was stunned into silence. There was absolutely no way he could get out of it, except by saying flatly that he was too scared to do it. It was true that he had logged up enough wins and places in point-to-points to be eligible for a permit; whether getting it at such short notice would prove as easy as Peter seemed to think was not a certainty, but the only slim chance he could see of getting out of it. Even the thought of the long drive over to Berkshire with Pip in the morning did nothing to allay his dismay. Romantic love did not mix with being shit-scared.

He could not totally hide that he was less than enchanted with his prospects.

'It's tough on Peter,' Pip said. 'He wanted to do it so much.'

Did she think his misery was for Peter? He agreed, so

115

that she would. She departed, and left Jonathan to a night of sleepless apprehension. At three o'clock in the morning the National fences took on diabolical dimensions and all the press photos he had ever seen of falling horses combined in his mind to thud into Bechers Brook like conkers off an autumn tree. He dozed, awoke, remembered, groaned. At six o'clock he answered the blaring of the alarm and stumbled out to feed his horse. It was freezing cold and raining, and the decaying house groaned and rattled about him as he mucked out. He went out to the well to fetch clean water, empty the wheelbarrow. Being Sunday made no difference, for Dogwood had no days off; they did not suit him. An hour later Jonathan was zipped up into his arctic anorak, rain dinning on his crash-helmet, riding stoically out through the park, his frozen fingers trying to contain his race-horse's eagerness.

It was then, the circulation beginning to get into its stride, that he began to warm not only physically but in the mental processes as well. Dogwood was a bloody good horse and no one knew his style better than himself. He wasn't entered in the National just for a lark; he was a National stamp of horse with the jumping ability and the staying power, and at that moment he felt like it. His great raking stride devoured the ground even at a walk; the exercise he had done back at Geoff's had been only a fraction of what he now did out of Mallow End, yet he was never tired and had a bloom on his winter coat like that on a summer filly. He always looked about him at exercise, never doddled along like some bored racehorses of Jonathan's acquaintance.

'I'm stupid,' Jonathan told himself, 'to be frightened.'

He would have liked a practice first, that's all. Or so he told himself. He decided it was an attitude of mind. He always felt himself that he lacked confidence, but other people never accused him of it. He covered up well, should have been an actor....

'Besides,' he said to Dogwood, 'I've got to.' It was quite

obviously one of those things you would never forgive yourself for turning down when it was too late to change your mind. Even if you fell at the first fence, you would have achieved a certain credibility by being game enough to start. It could be argued that it was safer than many a point-to-point, the competitors being experienced and proved. The longer he argued it in his mind the more convinced he was that his first panics had been unworthy. After all sixteen-year-olds had ridden in the National; Bruce Hobbs had won it at seventeen, and girls rode in it, commented upon not for their spirit but for their prettiness or otherwise. By the time he got home Jonathan felt a new man.

Pip was waiting for him, her Mini parked outside. The new man felt his old ardour stirring at the sight of her, and saw that the long car ride was full of possibilities.

'I've got to change, if I'm going to Portman Square,' he said. 'Got to look worthy and upstanding.'

'Okay. I'll do Dogwood, if you like, and you can get ready.'

She wasn't just a pretty face.

Jonathan got spruced up and they set out half an hour later. She asked him if he would prefer to drive, but he did not see that he had anything to prove in that line and turned the offer down. He got the heater working and checked the route on the road-map, making sure they avoided his own home town which was on the way. Then he settled back and wondered how to introduce the subject nearest to his heart, aware that there would never be a better opportunity. Once Peter was home he wouldn't get her to himself again.

If he could ride over Aintree, he could surely find the courage to say the right things to Pip? But he couldn't think of them. He fidgetted with the heater knobs. His brain had seized up. He was bloody hopeless.

'Left at the next roundabout,' he said.

Pip was frightened she would drive right off the road, the way she felt. She had lain awake all night thinking about Jonathan riding in the Grand National and sitting beside her in the Mini all the way to Berkshire, and her concentration was suffering badly from lack of sleep and Jonathan's close proximity. He was the only boy she had ever met to turn down her offer of driving. She wished he hadn't, for she wasn't in a fit state. Peter had already told her that girls threw themselves at Jonathan, but Peter teased most of the time, and Jonathan did not seem to be interested in girls. Peter said if they kissed and cuddled a bit in front of Jonathan it might stir him to jealousy, but Pip thought that was just Peter's larky way of getting a kiss himself.

Peter was a darling, but did not have the same effect on her as Jonathan did. Human nature being naturally perverse, she knew it was Jonathan's reserve that attracted her, the impression he gave of being very much his own man. There was also the mystery of his break with his family, which Peter said darkly was something only Jonathan himself could tell her, but if you knew his mother ... big grimaces of disapproval. Jonathan was not the sort of person one asked personal questions of, even when he was being cheerful and friendly. Quite often he was quiet and moody, but never bad-tempered, like her father, always kind and considerate.

'Oh, yes, he's a paragon', Peter agreed. 'He was kidnapped, did you know, and his parents had to pay half a million to get him back? He's had a tough life.'

'I don't believe you!' You could never tell with Peter.

'Don't, if you like. It's true though. It's tough proving you're worth half a million. He's never been convinced of it himself, that's why he gives you that brooding impression.'

With Peter's grin, how could you tell? The only thing Peter was really serious about was his career, and that was never a subject for jokes. But Jonathan did not seem to be contemplating a career, which seemed odd to Pip, when he was obviously extremely bright and well-educated.

'He's resting,' Peter said.

'Resting from what?'

'Having a hard time,' Peter said.

Curiouser and curiouser, thought Pip. But could not ask. Even now, when the opportunity for lengthy conversation was at hand, the road empty ahead, the car warm and cosy, she could not ask him any questions, although it would have seemed the most natural way of passing the journey. She was actutely aware of his presence, his silence, his unaccustomed appearance in clean shirt and tie for the Jockey Club authorities, his pale preoccupied profile, his lovely curls recently hacked back by Peter with the stable scissors ... the whole experience threatened to overwhelm her. And when she thought of him riding out for the big race—

'*Jesus Christ!*'

She heard Jonathan say it before she noticed what was happening. Startled, she came to in time to see a Ford Escort driven by a white-haired man coming out of a side-turning right across her path. He was looking the other way and kept on coming. Pip flung the wheel violently round and missed him by inches, but the Mini then went into an uncontrollable skid on the wet road. Pip knew not to touch the brake, but had no other ideas about correcting skids and clung on grimly, terrified, thinking she had killed both of them. The Mini went up the grass verge on the opposite side of the road, teetered wildly on the brink of a fair-sized ditch, and miraculously came to a halt without going over the edge. The Ford Escort, having seen nothing, was driving away ahead of them.

'Oh, Christ, I'm sorry!' Pip said, and burst into tears.

Jonathan had hit his head on something and was looking surprised, slumped back in his seat.

'Cor!' he said. 'And cor again!' He groaned, raised a grin, and said, 'Are you all right?'

Pip wept.

'Yes, I'd say,' Jonathan remarked, and handed over his best white handkerchief, intended to impress the Jockey Club.

'I'm sorry! I'm so sorry! You should have driven.'

'It wasn't your fault. That old dodderer! Although I suppose we'll be like that one day, creeping along at twenty miles an hour without looking.'

It was typical of Jonathan, Pip thought, to think of the old boy with sympathy instead of rage. He had been the nearest to being mashed, but was far calmer than she was. He got out to study the Mini and reported back that all seemed to be in place.

'You'll drive now,' Pip said eagerly, unclipping her seat-belt.

'Oh no, I won't,' he said.

He got back into the passenger seat.

'Please!'

'Certainly not. It's like getting back on a horse when it's just buried you—something that has to be done. The sooner the better. Up you get, dear, press on undaunted.'

'I am daunted.'

But she started up again and drove the Mini off the verge. It had a new rattle, but nothing worse. Pip felt terrible, especially at crying and fussing, and not keeping calm and witty in the face of fear which naturally her hero had done. She was quite sure his taste was for cool, brave girls, and she was disintegrating fast. She couldn't drive before the mishap, and now she was even less capable. Perhaps Jonathan sensed this, because he glanced at his watch and said, 'There's a decent pub about forty minutes on. We'll stop there for coffee and then I'll drive after that, if you like.'

'I didn't sleep last night, thinking about things. I wasn't in a fit state before, and now I'm worse.'

'What were you thinking about?'

'You, mainly,' Pip said.

After she had said it there was a long silence. Pip stared at the road wondering if she was out of her mind. The shock had unbalanced her. But it was all of a piece with the way she felt, she didn't care. She kept her eyes on the road, in case another old man drove out in front of her. If he did, she would hit him, for sure. Perhaps she had concussion.

'What about me?' Jonathan said eventually. 'Riding in the Grand National, you mean?'

'No. Really I mean—you—riding, or not riding.'

Long pause.

Then he said, 'I think about you a lot too, but I thought you had clicked with Peter.'

'There's nothing between Peter and me, only fun. Peter said he'd try and make you jealous.'

'I am jealous.'

Pip smiled. 'That's all right then.'

Jonathan did not say any more. Pip did not look at him, concentrating hard on her driving, which was necessary as they had come out on to an arterial approaching a town. Her head throbbed and she felt as if she had had too much to drink, but she felt relieved at what she had done. Life was too short to lose time in misunderstandings. So what if he wasn't interested? He was going soon anyway, she supposed. He was too polite to snub her directly, if he wasn't interested, but at least she had put the message over.

'It's straight over at the traffic lights, then left fork at the bottom. If there's a space to park we can stop at the Golden Lion—they do coffee.'

Jonathan was dangerously near home, but didn't care. He had hit his head in the near-accident and was thinking much the same as Pip—that concussion had brought on hallucinations. He was wary, frightened, and the spectre of Iris eight months pregnant terrified him. He was a free man, or so he had thought, and now he did not know. He had this doubt quite suddenly, unbidden. It came simultaneously with Pip's declaration of interest in him, to temper his instinctive joy.

There was a parking place and Pip drove neatly into it and turned off the engine. She looked nervous now, and embarrassed, and Jonathan wondered if he had understood her properly. They got out and locked the doors.

'You're okay, aren't you? Nothing damaged?'

Jonathan took her arm as they went into the hotel.

'You're not light-headed?'

She smiled. 'No.'

'If you said what—I—I think you said,' Jonathan said, with difficulty, 'it makes me very happy.'

'Good,' she said.

They sat down at a table in the lounge and a waitress took their order. Could it be true, Jonathan thought? He really did feel rather strange, as if he was dreaming, but nothing was out of place, and Pip was smiling. He knew he ought to say something smooth and loving, but his brain was empty. Stunned. He was smiling too; he could feel it growing, but no words to go with it.

Pip decided to go to the loo and Jonathan made an effort to pull himself together.

'I'm such a mess,' she said when she came back. 'I'm sorry I got the hysterics.'

'No—you coped very well. We're here, all in one piece, to prove it.'

He was glad it had happened, if the shock had compelled her amazing confession.

'It's all happening this week,' he said. 'All this and the National too! Are you sure Peter's interest in you is purely brotherly? I never got that impression.'

'Yes. It's a fact. He says he likes big fat girls with—I won't say it—it's too unromantic. He says I'm too skinny for him. But I'm very fond of him. He's just so nice.'

'Yes. I suppose he is.'

Never having given it much thought, Jonathan was bound to agree. 'Poor old devil! His collar-bone, I mean. I bet he's sick. He'll be in a foul temper. He's not nice the whole time, you know, not when things like this happen.'

'Not surprising! He's lived for that ride, thought of nothing else ever since I've known him.'

'That's right. That's why I came away with him, because he wanted to leave everything, and just take off with Dogwood. Just for the National, and nothing else. We've neither of us thought of anything else, not even what happens afterwards.'

Pip, dying to know what happened before, suggested, 'You worked with him?'

'Well—no. We lived near each other—at home, that is—then he went to work with his brother, and I—I joined him there when—'

His voice faded and he looked acutely unhappy.

'You had a row at home?'

'At school. I packed it in. I was supposed to be taking Oxford entrance. Something happened.'

He pushed back his chair suddenly and stood up.

'Let's go. I can't tell you, not now. It'll spoil everything.'

He drove the rest of the way, and Pip sat close to him, trying not to wonder what he had done. It was all wonderful, and she felt deliciously happy, and tired, and excited altogether, and wanted the journey to go on for ever.

Chapter 7

The timing of Jonathan and Pip's mutual declaration of love for each other was not exactly well-chosen, for after the momentous car journey to Berkshire they did not get another chance to pursue their romance. They drove the dizzy forty miles on to Geoff's establishment and plunged deeply into emotions of another sort altogether.

Peter was bad-tempered beyond belief, in pain from his collar-bone and sundry bruises and sick with disappointment about his ride. Geoff had obviously had a row with his wife and was in a worse mood than Peter, and the atmosphere was such that Jonathan suggested they went their various ways without delay, Pip and Peter back to Mallow End and himself to London.

'That is—if you think I should ride Dogwood. I would have thought it would be worth getting someone who knows what to do.'

Both Geoff and Peter disagreed with this, saying Dogwood was a cantankerous old devil with jockeys he did not know and had given a lot of trouble in the past.

'Wouldn't bloody start the last two times I ran him,' Geoff growled. 'Bolted going down to the start and chucked one jockey over the starter's Landrover. We don't want all that sort of trouble again.'

So Jonathan collected the required forms and set off for London on the motor-bike, thinking all the way of Peter in the car with Pip, his mind buzzing with what life suddenly had in store with him.

Before he knew it, he was on his way to Aintree in the

Hargreaves horse-box, driving it because Peter couldn't, Pip beside him and Peter the other side of Pip, trying to find how they got from the M11 on to the A1.

'No problem. They all get together after Huntingdon. Just follow your nose.'

'I thought you have to have a Heavy Goods licence to drive this lorry,' Pip remarked.

'Yes, you do.'

'Have you?' Pip asked Jonathan.

'No, but Peter has.'

'He's not driving.'

'No. Well, with luck, no one's going to ask.'

'He's got a permit to ride, that's the main thing,' Peter said. 'You can't have everything.'

'I'll show that if I'm stopped.'

'Yeah. Permission to navigate round Aintree.'

Peter, having resigned himself to his injury, had cheered up since the weekend. With Jonathan it had worked the other way: he had become progressively more apprehensive, wondering what the hell he had taken on. Now it was Friday, and the race was the next day, and he had distinct butterflies in the stomach every time he thought of it, which was nearly all the time. Driving the big lorry for the first time was also pretty nerve-wracking, although much easier now they were on the motorway. They aimed to get to Liverpool before dark, and had made an early start, packing all their gear into the plushy living-quarters in front of the horse-space. Pip had had a slight disagreement with her parents about going up in the lorry.

'I'm going as a worker! I'm not just a hanger-on. I've got to saddle the horse and lead him round the paddock—Peter can't do it with his crock arm.'

A distraught phone call from Geoff the night before also made it sound unlikely that he was going to put in an appearance, which made them definitely short-staffed. He was having either a nervous or a physical breakdown, but his brother was not sympathetic. He merely thought the timing was bad.

'Lucky we've got Pip, that's all I can say,' he had remarked to Jonathan. 'I can make the declaration and collect your saddle when you've weighed out but I can't do much else.'

He was using pain-killers, and Jonathan was suffering from some pills Peter had given him to get rid of a surplus half a stone overweight before Saturday. They looked a wan pair between them, but Dogwood looked fantastic.

'After all, he's got to do most of the work,' Pip said.

Peter said, 'Jonathan's got to do a fair amount. You can spend Saturday morning in the sauna—that's what a lot of the jockeys do.'

'Like hell I will,' Jonathan said indignantly. 'If I do that I shall be clapped out, I'll fall off before the start.'

He had knocked off his cups of tea and hunks of bread and cheese and considered that sacrifice enough. He thought the sweat of pure fear would do the rest before the flag fell.

The weather was reasonable, not exactly springlike, but not threatening snow or frost either. It was the normal raw cold of early spring, the sky overcast, the air damp and still, good by racing standards. The big windscreen wipers beat rhythmically backwards and forwards, clearing the dirty spray that was flung up by every passing car and speeding lorry. Jonathan was not in a hurry, anxious not to spur his adrenalin to action, to save it all until it mattered.

Peter was poring over some tattered road-maps trying to work out their route.

'Go west, young man,' he muttered. 'Derby, I think. Left turn somewhere near Stamford.'

It was warm, cosy, in the cab. They stopped once for a coffee and sausage rolls, found the M6 early in the afternoon and approached industrial Lancashire with a sense of pilgrimage. The grey drizzle greased the roads; factory chimneys, water coolers, pylons fretted the skyline.

Peter anxiously scoured the road signs and Jonathan worked hard at giving Dogwood a smooth ride as the traffic built up and they were into local roads and roundabouts and traffic lights. He had got the hang of the lorry all right but was weary and losing concentration.

'It's coming up, by those traffic lights,' Peter said. 'Cross the lights and there's a left turn. Pretty narrow, as I remember it. You'll have to pull out to get in.'

The lights were red. They waited.

'I've never seen a racecourse in a place like this before,' Pip remarked.

'It was country once, when it started,' Peter said. 'Eighteen thirty something.'

The entrance was a gritty lane between awkward fences, twisting into a grassy opening in front of the stables. Several large horse-boxes were parked, and there was a field beyond full of cars, and more horse-boxes beyond that. The stables were built of old red brick, low and grey-roofed, rows and rows of them opening off lanes of black grit. When they went to explore, clutching their passes, they were lost in a maze of yards. Racing was in progress and horses were coming and going and being washed down, walked out to cool off. Lads and girls, hurried and over-worked, led out immaculate beasts, carted basketsful of gear and buckets of water and got shouted at by little bandy men in flat caps; the atmosphere was a comfort, familiar; it was always the same, whatever the course, the same people, the same conversation. The three of them were comforted by the familiarity. Jonathan tried to convince himself it was just another point-to-point, in essence ... he felt himself apart from the other two, his place out on the other side of the fence where the loudspeaker commentary could be heard coming and going in the rain and the crowd groaned, roared ... tomorrow was the climax of three days of racing.

'When racing's finished, we'll walk the course,' Peter said. 'We'll get Dogwood comfortable first.'

Some of the boxes had the names of past winners and the date painted on their doors. The one allocated to Dogwood had no such distinction, but the horse walked in and snuffled around in his usual nosey way. His ears were pricked and his eyes bright, the racing scene to his liking. He whinnied to his neighbours, pleased to be back in company. They unloaded his gear into the cupboard built across one corner of the box, gave him a net of hay.

'We'll walk him out after the racing, stretch his legs a bit,' Peter said.

The last race was over. The rain had stopped and a silvery light gleamed on the factories across the great, dun dereliction of the Aintree acres. The crowds streamed out from the stands, the litter blew aimlessly on the cold wind. Jonathan watched it all, feeling a bit like Dogwood, ears pricked and eyes bright; it all mattered like nothing had ever mattered before, the way he felt. Past challenges dwindled to child's play. The nervousness made him feel strange, apart from the other two. He tried to tell himself it was a nothing: every year a dozen or so inexperienced jockeys like himself faced the same day with equal trepidation; even the old hands were said to be strung up beforehand. He was, he told himself, in a very happy situation compared with most, having no ambitious trainer or fortune-seeker owner breathing down his neck. If he was destined to fall at the first, there would be no one to care very much, save Peter and Pip. He doubted if anyone would bet on him, so he had no responsibilities in that direction. He had nothing, in fact, to worry about at all. He shivered.

Peter looked at him and grinned.

'Shall we go?'

They were not the only ones walking the course. Streams of spectators and interested parties wanted a preview of the famous fences, but Jonathan walked alone, unaware of the company. The Grand National course overlapped the ordinary Aintree course only at the start and finish. The horses had to go round twice, a distance of over four and a half miles, and jump thirty jumps, all of which were far bigger and more solid than the biggest jumps on any other racecourse. The biggest jumps were five feet high and had ditches six feet wide on the take-off side. One of these was the third jump, and Jonathan, looking at it, thought that if he survived this one, and the stampede over the two preceding, he would have something to chalk up whatever might happen thereafter. There were over forty runners, and some of the jumps were none too wide; to get a clear view would be a bonus, let alone elbow room. The famous Becher's Brook looked unexpectedly innocuous on the approach, but the drop behind wasn't nice at all; Jonathan stood looking, hunched into his anorak. Some girls were standing against it having their photographs taken. Even with their arms raised up over their heads they did not break the skyline of solid spruce-covered wall. They looked at Jonathan and giggled, held out the camera.

'Will you take us, so we can all be in it? They'll never believe us at home. Isn't it awful? Fancy asking a poor horse to jump this!'

It looked even worse through the view-finder. Jonathan took the photo and handed the camera back, pulled himself together. At speed, on a sixteen-hand horse, it would be quite different. Dogwood would ping it. The next, narrow and at an angle, was not inviting. This was where, several years earlier, the whole field had piled up and the winner was the only horse so far behind that he was able to pick his way through the carnage when he got to it and continue on his way. This side of the course was flanked on the outside by a high embankment and a railway siding, piles of coal and corrugated iron fencing. Where the railway crossed a canal at the top end, the race-course abruptly left-handed to avoid going into the water, and continued alongside the canal, which was shut off by a fence (once horses had galloped into it). Drab housing shut off further views.

'The trouble with jumps this high,' Peter said, 'is that you can't see what's on the other side.'

'Bodies, you mean?'

'Yes. Unless you're in the lead, of course, when it doesn't matter.'

'Makes it more *interesting*.'

They walked on, heading for the factory chimneys with the sun coldly sinking behind them. Jonathan, mesmerized by the obstacles, remembered that he had to choose the best ground, and realized he would have to go round again. Tomorrow morning ... a good way to deploy the time.

'Just in case you're in front, second time round, make navigational notes,' Peter said. 'It's a bit messy up here, where the other courses cross.'

Jonathan, optimistically, noted. He did not linger long at the Chair, the biggest fence of all in front of the stands, but walked up the long, long run-in pretending he could hear the cheers, trying to guess what it must feel like. With luck he might finish. All the finishers got a cheer of some sort. He could not chat, or make any sort of effort, and Peter and Pip walked together, relatively carefree, even laughing. Peter had got over his outsize depression. His disappointment was just part of the everyday stuff of racing. If you couldn't take it, there was no point in trying to be a jockey. Racing was disappointments all the way. He who expects nothing, Jonathan thought carefully, and a sudden, wild splinter of his being pictured himself winning, and heard the famous roar of the Aintree crowd. He stopped, closed his eyes, pretending, felt himself smiling. When he came to, all he could hear was the evening skylarks and the bleat of a factory hooter for knocking-off time and he knew he was just as frightened as he had been when the idea of his riding had first been raised. This time tomorrow it would be over.

They went back to the lorry. They were going to sleep in it, and Pip's mother had stocked them up with home-made pies. Pip lit the small oven and put them in to warm. Peter said to Jonathan, 'You're not eating, fatso—you've still got to get some off.'

'Christ, I'm starving!'

Pip had thoughtfully brought the family scales and Jonathan tried them. He was still six pounds over what Dogwood had to carry. Peter and Pip gave him a lean plateful, no pastry or potatoes.

'A proper jockey wouldn't even have that,' Peter said severely.

'I never volunteered for this job.'

Peter then gave him a look which revealed the feelings that he had been successfully covering up, and Jonathan felt bad and shut up, and ate what he was given. They wouldn't allow him more than half a cup of tea. He felt hard done by, all the same, and went out to do Dogwood so that he wouldn't have to watch them eating chocolate mousse and Mars bars.

Tomorrow it would all be over. Not only the race, but his present career, if such it could be called. Tomorrow he would have to start thinking. He did not want to leave Pip. But there would be no reason for staying. He could not face the thought of going home. He groomed Dogwood, taking out his despairs on the horse's muscled frame. In the electric light Dogwood's coat had a shine on it like a new Rolls Royce; he was lean and hard and fighting fit. If the punters bet on looks, he would be carrying plenty of money tomorrow.

'You old devil, you! Just you look after me, you old fool. I want to live.'

He spun out the time, not wanting to be with the others, took Dogwood for a walk outside and a bite of grass, took him back and fed him, checked over his gear, mooched around looking at the opposition. It was dark and a few stars were scratching through the cloud. Jonathan walked down to the start of the course and prayed a bit, and then went back to the horse-box and straight to bed.

He supposed he slept some of the night, but it did not feel like it. He was aware two hours before Pip's alarm clock went off. At seven o'clock he had to ride Dogwood out on the course, the only exercising time allotted to the day's runners, and he gathered that the press turned out to make their last assessments of looks and vitality. Of the horse only, Jonathan hoped wildly, feeling fifty years old at least. Peter and Pip nobly rolled out of their bunks to accompany him: the lorry was freezing cold and condensation ran down the windows. Rubbing a hole, Jonathan peered out to see a grey but not exactly hopeless dawn, a vague pearly sunlight filtering in from the direction of Bechers. Peter made coffee and Pip went out to start getting Dogwood ready. Jonathan sat on his bunk looking at his feet, wondering how on earth he was going to get through the nine hours or so until the race.

A surprising number of people were out and about when he went to fetch his horse. Nearly all the jockeys were there to exercise, the famous and the not so famous, and several of them were kindly, his face being new, and quite a few people commented on Dogwood's looks. The horse felt like dynamite, and Jonathan was wholly occupied with not making a fool of himself. He got in behind a steady bunch and did a cautious canter with them, feeling the excitement bunched ominously between his knees, quivering in his hands, as Dogwood found himself once more in company. The air was sharp as the pace increased. Jonathan's eyes were watering, and the excitement was infectious, the feel of Dogwood's power cheered him enormously. If only they were going down to the start now, he thought!

Peter and Pip were waiting for him when he got back and took the horse solicitously. When Dogwood was fed they cooked Jonathan a boiled egg for his breakfast and waited on him kindly. It was only half-past eight and he felt as if he had been up for hours. Peter went out and bought some newspapers, and Jonathan read a few comments about Dogwood ('literally a dark horse' ... 'a fine jumper but extremely unreliable temperament' ... 'once a good horse but an unknown quantity since training upsets....') He rolled back into his bunk and stared at the ceiling. He had to groom Dogwood and walk the course again to pick the best ground, but there would still be hours ... it was already the longest day of his life, and nothing had even started.

Inexorably the time passed.

Jonathan disappeared down the course, not wanting any company. Pip and Peter went out to the yard and discussed the afternoon's tactics. Peter had to stand in as trainer which left Pip with the task of taking Dogwood to the paddock—no sinecure, as he pulled like a train during the preliminaries.

'You'll have to lead him in the parade too. I'll walk with you, but I can't do much about holding him,' Peter told her.

They were short-handed, but at least there was only one horse to cope with. They checked everything they could think of and every strap and buckle of the tack, and then sat in a patch of sunlight outside the box watching the comings and goings. New horses were arriving to join the overnight stayers, and Dogwood kept whinneying, restless in his box. The weather was improving, the clouds breaking up, and the first-comers were trickling in across the course and into the stands, and trailing away across the road towards Bechers with their picnic bags and thermoses, stools and transistor radios.

Peter looked at his watch for the umpteenth time.

'Just at the moment,' he said, 'I'm quite glad it's not me after all.'

When the time came, Pip found herself too pressed to worry. Jonathan had long since disappeared into the portals of the changing-room and when Peter departed for

133

the same building to collect the saddle she was left with her hands full, Dogwood storming out of his box to do battle as if he had been shut up for a month. She left when two other horses nearby set off, determined to follow them and do whatever they did, feeling desperately inexperienced in this professional atmosphere after the easy informality of the point-to-point meetings. Following was difficult, as Dogwood was set to overtake everything in sight, his walk—restrained—turning into a succession of pirouettes as his quarters went ahead faster than his battened-down front end. She was nearly lifted off her feet, but won the battle not to overtake, although the horse in front was looking understandably alarmed at the antics going on behind him. The crowds round the paddock were dense and the paddock was too small to take all the runners, although Dogwood dragged her in willy-nilly. There was no sign of Peter and the saddle, so she was forced to lead Dogwood round through the crush, stopping and starting, her hair falling over her face and sticking in strands to her sweaty cheeks. Dogwood might qualify for the best-turned out horse, but this 'lad' was a non-starter. She heard several people comment on his looks and ask who he was but she had no breath to answer with. All the saddling boxes seemed to be full, but she kept her eyes sharply in that direction and at last saw Peter emerge out of the crowd with Jonathan's saddle over his arm. She barged her way out of the paddock and made in his direction and they were lucky enough to coincide at a box whose inmate was just departing. Peter grinned.

'Still in one piece?'

'The horse is. I don't know about me.'

Peter started to strip off the rugs with his good arm and Pip stood at Dogwood's head, holding him on both sides of the bit. Looking out towards the crowd, she saw a woman staring at them from the mound of grass between the boxes and the paddock. She looked, for a second, startlingly familiar, although Pip knew she did not know her. She was tall and autocratic-looking, smartly dressed in tweeds. She started to come towards them.

'Peter!'

Peter turned round and his mouth dropped.

'*Bloody hell*!'

Pip was startled by his reaction.

'It's Jonathan's mother!'

The woman had negotiated the fence with a surprising agility and was now alongside, looking grim.

'I take it this is the horse Jonathan is riding?'

Peter busied himself with the girth, muttering something.

'Why Jonathan?'

'I was going to ride him. I've broken my collar-bone.'

'I was reading the paper over breakfast—the list of runners. I nearly had a fit when I saw Jonathan's name. I drove straight up here.'

'You're not going to stop him!'

'No. But perhaps you would tell him to consider his neck, as he is now the father of a daughter.'

Peter straightened up abruptly.

'You *shit*!' he said.

'I beg your pardon?' Mrs Meredith's voice was icy.

'Just keep out of his way until it's over! It's no time to tell him now! Leave us alone!'

Mrs Meredith actually smiled. 'Your manners haven't improved one jot, Peter. I appreciate your concern, but I am depending upon you to tell Jonathan the news, before or after the race—that's quite immaterial. And point out that there are certain duties he owes to a good many people, not least himself. He can't run away all his life. Tell him I would like to see him before he leaves here. I'll be in the members' bar after the last race.'

She walked away back towards the stands, leaving Peter and Pip steam-rollered.

'Did she say—he—he's a *father*?' Pip said faintly.

'Yeah—that's what I gathered.'

'He's not married, is he?'

'Christ, no! Look, forget it, Pip. As if he hasn't got enough—having that for a mother, and bloody Iris, and riding in the Grand National. . . .' Peter was almost sobbing, heaving at the girth, wincing with his collar-bone. 'She's a shit, the biggest—blast it—'

'Peter—'

'Do you wonder he's a bit—well, how he is?'

'No. But that girl—what's her name?—Iris, you said—'

'Oh, shut up. Is the breast-plate okay?'

'Yes. The number cloth's rucked up your side.'

'We'll leave his rugs. The sun's shining.'

'Nearly everybody else has gone—'

'There's tons of time. The jockeys aren't out yet.'

'They're coming now.'

'Take him then. I'll go and meet Jonathan,. Don't say anything! God, I hope he doesn't see her!'

Dogwood plunged out of the box, and Pip got towed back to the paddock where she tried to lead Dogwood round, but there were too many people in the way. She did not know whether she was coming or going . . . Jonathan a *father*! What sort of a joke was that? Dogwood barged a smart-looking owner and she apologized. The bell rang for mounting, but she couldn't even see Jonathan.

She felt like weeping, and the day's excitement hadn't even started yet.

Suddenly Jonathan and Peter were at her side, actually smiling. Pip felt a wild flush of emotion for her lovely Jonathan, father or no father, and knew for a moment that she was united with his terrible mother in thinking only of his safety. But she managed to show a cool front (she hoped), biting her lip to stop herself saying anything stupid.

'Thank God the waiting's over,' he said. 'That's the worst bit of all. Everybody said the same.'

He tightened the girths and Peter gave him a leg-up with his good arm. The crowd was fighting its way back to the stands and the horses started to leave the paddock. They made one circuit, waiting for room, then they were away through a sea of staring faces across the grass towards the gates on to the course. Pip led Dogwood, more settled now that his rider was aboard, and Peter walked on the other side, ready to help if necessary. They had to parade in front of the stands, and the stewards were trying to get them in number order as they went through on to the course. Dogwood was number sixteen and they got shouted at to hurry. Several horses pulled up to allow them past. Pip ran, and Dogwood plunged at her side, kicking out in all directions, feeling his hooves on the thick green turf and seeing the wide galloping spaces opening out before him. Jonathan calmed him, sitting still and talking to him, and he settled into his right place and they heard his named called by the commentator as he sidled down in front of the buzzing stands. Pip thought of Mrs Meredith standing there watching, and felt sick.

They had to turn and come back, and then the horses were let off their leads, and went bucketting away down past the start to stretch their legs as far as the first fence. Pip reached up to undo the clip.

'Good luck! Look after yourself!'

She saw Jonathan's expression, oblivious of her, Peter and everyone else in the world, looking between Dogwood's pricked ears to the horses breaking away ahead of him, anticipating Dogwood's plunging acceleration.

'Next to go down is number sixteen—that's Dogwood, ridden by Mr J. Meredith....'

He went like a jet-powered missile, disappearing round the bend as if he thought he was in the Derby.

'Jesus! I hope he can stop!' Peter said.

They got out of the way and stood on the rails, watching. It was all out of their hands now. There were horses everywhere, some coming back, some still going down, lads and trainers retreating. The start area was large but looked uncomfortably crowded, the jockeys circling nervously, taking up their tactical positions, the most confident on the inside, the optimistic ruck on the wide outside, in no hurry. The starter was standing by his platform.

Pip and Peter saw Dogwood come back, much to their relief, still pulling, but well in hand. He seemed to be behaving himself and they decided to try and elbow their way into the stand to get some chance of seeing the race, which was now the ambition of all their fellow-helpers. Struggling and shoving for elbow-room, they heard the commentator's tense announcement, 'They're under starter's orders!' Straggling across the whole width of the course the untidy line began to move forwards. The crowd murmured. The sun came out from behind a cloud and gleamed on the bright colours. The tapes sprang up. The crowd's roar went up—'They're off!'—and seemed to power the field with its breath, blasting them into the bend at what seemed a terrifying pace.

Pip groaned and clutched Peter's bad arm, but he did not notice the pain, adrift on his own agonized longing to be where Jonathan was. It was almost more than he could bear, to see the horses go. Bloody *lucky* Jonathan, who had not even wanted!... Peter could have cried, or spat, as the frenzied drumming of hooves faded away round the bend and the skylarks twittered in excitement overhead.

Chapter 8

Jonathan had got Dogwood near the outside as it seemed more prudent but as there were so many horses taking up the same place he found himself without any daylight when the great mass of horseflesh started to move inexorably forward. It meant he was going to be at the back when they got to the first jump and the horse would not get a clear view, but it was better than being squashed in the front rank and perhaps knocked for six through sheer overcrowding.

Dogwood went without his having to do anything, pulling so violently that he almost got wrenched out of the saddle. He was hard on the bunched quarters ahead of him, oblivious to the starter's 'Steady, jockeys, at the front!' Jonathan never saw the tape at all, only the bank of horseflesh bounding forward, tight frightened ears pricked to the sky, the gaudy colours jerked into motion. He felt the immense strength of his own horse lift him, heard the sudden thrilling pounding of hooves. His right leg was crushed against another momentarily; stirrups clinked, a curse, the straining of girth and leather and the tremendous pulling of Dogwood against his sweaty hands, almost more than he could contain ... still no daylight, and only the recollection Fthat it was two furlongs to the first fence to comfort him. There was very little else. The speed was hair-raising, the sense of having no control over circumstances, although not unexpected, was as unpleasant as he had guessed it might be. Sheer animal power dominated, the men as flimsy by comparison as their butterfly silks, praying to survive this wild initiation and ride on to calmer pastures.

Jonathan, having told himself he would feel all right once the tapes had gone up, now realized that this was a myth, and postponed all hope of well-being until after the first fence. He could see nothing ahead of him but backs and buttocks, a glimpse of the high iron gateways shutting off the Melling road, of giant hoardings ... somewhere in front of him five foot of solid thorn hedge was lying in wait—God, it must be soon! The vibrations of pounding hooves filled the universe.

The horse ahead of him changed shape, launching skywards. Jonathan, ready for it, felt Dogwood's momentary check of surprise, the quick, self-preserving extra stride, and then they were airborne, magnificently, better than all dreams, Dogwood's powerful quarters catapulting them over the obstacle with startled generosity. He let out an indignant grunt on landing, and Jonathan heard himself laugh. It was relief, elation, after the funk. To have gone at the first—that would have been disappointment insupportable—but disaster was not for him. Carnage was all round: a face showed terror somewhere in the region of Dogwood's knees, and there was a horse sideways on, scrabbling for its feet, which Dogwood swerved round adroitly. The air was filled with the cracking of fierce twigs and the thudding of fallers, but Jonathan had found daylight. The course was visible ahead, a green river of turf, the next jump unequivocally in view ... no excuses now.

Jonathan took a pull at Dogwood. The pace seemed to him very hot with four miles ahead but perhaps he was no judge of that. He was by no means up with the leaders but at least he now had some visibility, a most desirable improvement. The run to the second was brief and, surprised by the solidity of the first, Dogwood stood off and jumped with great respect, tucking up his legs. Jonathan, with a second burst of midair elation, remembered that the third was one of the killers ... but being able to actually see it must be to his advantage ... bearing down on it, he was not so sure. It was solid as rock and the ditch was like an elephant trap. He felt Dogwood's amazement, hesitation. He sat into him with all his strength, driving with his back and legs, heard the clonking and crashing as the first horses hit its top and saw the backsides flying, white breeches and swirling tails. Dogwood landed heavily and pecked but greater jockeys than Jonathan were in worse straits. Somebody rolled under Dogwood's hooves and the horse, one stride out of his stumble, side-stepped and stumbled for a second time, almost coming to a halt.

Jonathan, holding on by willpower, heard himself swearing. The reins were out to the knot and he hauled them in like washing, getting back hold of Dogwood's head and urging him on. They had lost several lengths. There were a lot of horses ahead of him but quite a lot of disaster behind and two loose horses matily alongside, not at all where he wanted them. Two more fences to Becher's and he wasn't frightened any more. They were vast and solid but Dogwood had got the measure of what was expected of him and jumped big. The loose horses went ahead. The horse inside him was ridden by the current champion jockey and was lobbing along looking as if he knew exactly what he was doing, but Jonathan, not a champion, did not particularly want to jump Bechers on the inside where the drop was bigger and edged his horse over slightly towards the centre. The approach to Bechers was innocuous enough after what they had already faced. Poor trusting old Dogwood! Jonathan took a steadying pull at him, not wanting him to stand off—there was too far to go on the other side—but Dogwood was not much wanting to be dictated to. He tugged at the bit but met the obstacles by sheer good fortune on a perfect stride. Jonathan let the reins run, soaring into space. It was fantastic, seeing clear ahead and feeling the momentary calm, the wind knifing his sweat, sweet silence, suspension, before the moment of touch-down. A shivering split-second of agony of landing, feeling the elastic pasterns taking the shock, on tenterhooks for keeling over out of sheer amazement ... but no, Dogwood staggered away back into action, lengthening, pulling, steady as a rock.

The champion jockey was now by his superior tactics some three lengths ahead and there was a fair herd still beyond, although many of the horses appeared to have no riders. They were just far enough ahead to give a comforting sense of still being in the race with them, but not too close for comfort. Jonathan dreaded having to jump close behind another horse, of getting hemmed in. He could hear hooves behind him but what he could not see he was not going to bother about. A head came up alongside; the next jump was there and he jumped it upsides with his companion and realized he had made it to the Canal turn. Things would happen fast after that, he remembered. He must keep his cool and Dogwood must answer the helm.

A bank of gawping faces swept up on the near side and a horse came up fast, too close, cutting off Jonathan's opportunity of swinging into the jump on an angle to take the right-hand bend beyond. Blasting to himself, Jonathan gave Dogwood the boot to jump nicely off it.

There was a horse sitting like a surprised rabbit on the other side and a jockey running fast. Jonathan had to keep straight on to avoid them, and carried another horse on his off side with him. With blasphemy all about him, he swung Dogwood left-handed as hard as he could—too hard, checking him in his stride and putting him off-balance. Damn and blast! Offended, the horse was bucketing down the short run towards Valentine's with his head in the air just where he needed total concentration. The other jockey, more experienced, turned neatly and went a length ahead and the fallen horse joined Jonathan alongside so that he had no choice but to go on the heels of the one ahead. Dogwood had got the bit between his teeth and flung himself at the stark face of Valentine's with more eagerness than skill, hitting the top hard and scattering spruce in all directions. Jonathan got a whiff of resinous pine in his nostrils—like bloody Christmas, all we need is candles, he thought!—light-headed with his amazing progress. Landing jerked him back to sense, crashing his spine nearly out of the back of his neck. He grunted with shock, wondering if he would hold together as long as Dogwood.

But nobody behind was overtaking him—yet—and he seemed, by pure good luck, to be travelling nicely in the rear of the ten or so who were in business. Dogwood now knew what sort of obstacles he was facing; his rider had cast off his early panics and felt confidence flooding in to take their place. He even, momentarily, felt the bright sunshine on his lifted face and smelt with pleasure the hot familiar smell of hard-pressed horse and soapy leather. Dogwood was still pulling characteristically, his blood roused, his long loppy ears pricking and switching back alternately, as if to enquire, 'What the hell are we doing, mate?' But he felt good, in no way in disagreement. He felt fresh and strong and anxious to get on with it, and Jonathan for the first time thought that there was, perhaps, a chance that he was not going to disgrace himself after all.

Peter could not get the binoculars to focus, or else his fingers were trembling too much. The loudspeaker had not mentioned Dogwood once, not as a faller nor as a back-marker, nor even as one amongst the first dozen or so.

'He's bloody vanished,' he muttered to Pip.

'If he's a faller he'd have said. He tries to tell you all the fallers.'

There was enough of them, a wincing recital of familiar names. Geoff's colours were unfamiliar and perhaps even the renowned Peter O'Sullevan had not thought them worth memorizing.

'We'll see soon,' Pip said. She was pressed close to him, shaking like a leaf. 'It's awful,' she said. 'I never guessed I'd feel—' There wasn't a word for what she felt like.

The horses were somewhere out by Anchor Bridge, way

down in the country and virtually out of sight. There were no jumps down there until the two that were within sight coming up towards the stands, two fairly innocuous ones before the awesome Chair.

'We'll see when they come round the bend,' Pip said. 'Get focused on the first of those two jumps. Look for the colour of his cap.'

Peter could not even remember what colour it was.

'Orange,' she said, as if she knew.

'Oh, Jesus,' Peter said.

'They have crossed the Melling road for the second time and are coming round the turn now. Penrose is in the lead closely followed by Great Bear, and after Great Bear comes Manic, Elderberry Wine, Scintillate, No Answer, followed by Lacquer and Persephone and Maggie's Choice. After Maggie's Choice is the grey Pigeon Pie, Bradwell Creek and Dogwood making up ground....'

Pip screamed. Peter dropped the binoculars but scooped them up with his good arm before they hit the ground. He was shaking too much to use them.

'You can see him now—the orange cap—'

'Outside the grey—'

The hum from the stands as the horses came into view crescendoed steadily as the commentator's voice quickened and rose with excitement. The shock of hearing that Dogwood was still in the race was followed in Peter's mind by an explosive thrust of pure hate towards Jonathan for stealing his glory; his instinctive jealously brought a groan to his lips which he could not compress. To be riding that horse now ... over the second of the two comparatively innocuous jumps that preceded the Chair in front of the stands—that he had missed this unique and glorious opportunity was as painful as anything he had ever experienced. It happened to proper jockeys all the time, he remembered; the rider of the favourite had been put out by a fall at Wincanton only the evening before. But it did not help the pain, seeing Dogwood's plugging gallop as he approached the Chair, his chunky familiar frame on the heels of the renowned Great Bear and famous No Answer, his scruffy little mane flying and his ears cocked as the white wings loomed, seeing old Jonathan sitting there as if he wasn't scared out of his mind at all, heels driving, hands forward, mouth wide open ... Peter shut his eyes at the moment of take-off, heard Pip gasp.

'Maggie's Choice is a faller! Penrose is clear and so is Great Bear and Manic and Scintillate and No Answer. Dogwood has jumped it and behind Dogwood is Bradwell Creek and Lodestone and then ten, twelve lengths behind is Silver Coin and behind Silver Coin is Maytree and those are all that are in with a chance now. Coming to the water it's Penrose and Great Bear and....'

Peter opened his eyes to see Dogwood kicking off a branch of spruce entangled in his tail and belting towards the water which was right in front of where they were standing. They were close now, close enough to see how hard Dogwood was still pulling, to see the grimace on Jonathan's face as he stood off and took off a full stride too soon, sailing over the water with a vast, extravagant leap that lost him two lengths on the nippy No Answer, the class favourite who knew all about Aintree and was wasting no energy. Behind them on the wind came the receding frenzy of pounding hooves. They belted round the sharp bend at the top of the course and made out into the country again for the second circuit, shedding loose horses at the stable gates, passing returning jockeys from the first jump who stood and watched them go by, thinking ... God, thought Peter, as bad as me! They could feel no more envy than he did, balefully overlaying his joy at Dogwood's progress.

Guessing, Pip put out an arm and hugged him suddenly, and reached up and kissed him, and turned back to watch the depleted field come to the first jump for the second time. It was now called number seventeen, and was no smaller than the first time round save for a few dents in the top. The stand buzzed with the passing excitement, conjecture, amazement ... the commentator reported progress, but there were no more fallers, the survivors having learned the score. Some stragglers went on by and were encouraged, and disappeared across the kicked dirt on the Melling road, disheartened but game. To finish was a triumph of its own, even if the cheers were half a mile ahead.

Jonathan's mood had changed by the time they were starting the second circuit. Plain amazement at their joint prowess and the wild elation it had inspired were now replaced by a dour sense of determination. To make a mistake now would be far more painful than it might have been earlier. It all mattered now, when before it had been a wild and unlikely adventure. Dogwood had lost his initial steam but still felt good; his jockey was not so sure, his shoulders aching and his thighs beginning to weaken when they were going to be needed more urgently than before. But *girls* did it now, he reminded himself sternly. Dogwood twitched an ear back to him and he spoke to it. 'Keep it up, old boy. You're doing a treat.'

The big ditch and fence two before Bechers yawned, needing all their joint effort. Jonathan, in mid-air, found he was back with the champion jockey again, but the champion jockey did not look tired and sat like a rock as his horse pecked on landing, picking him up with far more skill than Jonathan suspected Dogwood would receive if he did the same thing.

'Who are you?' the champion jockey asked him as they galloped to the next but, his horse jumping with the same professional economy he had shown earlier on the course, he was two lengths before Jonathan could remember what his own name was. They were coming to Bechers second time round, and there were five horses ahead of him and two on his heels. This was where trouble was likely, most of the horses by now tiring fast. Some of them had good memories too. Three of them refused, two right in front of Jonathan, and one horse ahead fell. Jonathan had no time at all in which to rethink or change direction. The nearest refuser turned in his direction to run across, saw him coming and hesitated fractionally. Jonathan had a glimpse of its glazed eye and blood-filled nostril and its jockey's face buried right up in its mane between its ears. His foot caught the horse's shoulder as Dogwood took off, knocking him slightly off balance, so he went over this time with a heart-stopping curiosity as to whether he was still going to be poised over the saddle at the bottom of the long plunge down or over Dogwood's ears instead. The view down was not comforting either, heads rolling below and the flash of upturned hoofs, polished by the firm grass, flailing just where they wanted to go. Dogwood gave a convulsive paddle behind and landed a couple of inches clear of the faller but whether his hind legs cleared the disaster area Jonathan could not tell. The effort to avoid his fellow caused him to land badly and it was touch and go for Jonathan as to whether he stayed aboard. They staggered up the bank together. Jonathan bit his lip painfully and Dogwood snorted and grunted in his usual indignant way as he gathered himself together.

There were now only three horses in front of him. Jonathan could not believe his luck. The possibilities could unnerve him if he did not concentrate. Nothing mattered now but helping Dogwood, not straying off into cloud-cuckoo-land. Dogwood was plugging away manfully but how much steam he had left Jonathan could not tell. He was no longer pulling, but he seemed to be going easily in the circumstances. Jonathan was desperately out of breath and guessed he was failing fast but pure euphoria had him in its grip. Nobody could ever guess, he thought, what it felt like ... the course virtually empty ahead of him and *two* Bechers behind! It was rather like being drunk, the mind reeling. The sun shone gloriously, he could even hear the skylarks, and shreds of the commentary blowing down the wind. Down the course the factory windows sparkled like diamonds.

'We—are—bloody good—Dogwood!' he chanted.

There was all the room in the world at the Canal turn. He could pick his course, swing left-handed into the jump without a thought for his fellow men, for they had all vanished. Up and over, and out facing in the right direction ...bloody Valentines! he had forgotten the hazards still to come. Unlike Bechers from the approach, Valentines looked as high as a house. No, it was all in the mind; it was only two inches higher ... something to do with the way the light fell. Or was his mind going? No, his mind had already gone, to be here at all. He rode into it, driving Dogwood hard, looking for a good stride. Dogwood lenghtened, flew. They were up into the bluey, the cold wind, spruce flying, sweat and lather spittling the blue sky. Coming down, the impact rattled his bones, made him realize with a shock how weak his muscles had become as he endeavoured to hold Dogwood together and drive him on. And yet Dogwood felt good, responded, took a strong hold and pounded forward, ears pricked. There was still a mile to go, but they were gaining on the horses ahead. Jonathan could not believe his eyes. He was going to get another chance to tell the champion jockey his name—or, with luck, the champion jockey might find out without his ever saying a word ... he would read it in the newspapers.

'Come on, Dogwood, we're in with a chance!'

Dogwood's long ear picked up his choking voice. It switched back, and forward to the next jump. Over that perfectly and then it was the big one looming. Dogwood gave a little snort, shortened his stride to get it right, reached for it.

It was as if the lights went out, the sun blew up.

148

'Something's happened,' Peter said. 'I can't see him.'

'You can't see any of them from here. Not yet. the commentator never said—'

'There's a faller anyway, the ditch after Valentine's.'

It was so far away, even the binoculars could only make out spots, people running, cars moving. Nobody else cared, watching the specks that were the three leaders, listening to the inexorable voice which no longer mentioned Dogwood.

'But he never *said*! He must have noticed—'

'No, he's watching the leaders. He can't see everything. But he's not there, Dogwood I mean.'

He was trying to pick up the loose horses in the binoculars, but none of them seemed to be Dogwood. He wouldn't say it, but all was ominous stillness at the ditch after Valentine's. The people were drifting there, attracted. By what? The sudden change of fortune was chilling.

'He might have refused, or pulled up. He never expected to get so far, did he?'

Pip was being terribly sensible, so as not to scream and cry. Her heart was knocking like a played-out engine.

'It's so far away!'

'Let's go, shall we?' Peter said suddenly. 'They're not coming, not that I can see.'

The leaders were coming and the crowd was beginning the famous buzz of excitement that would lead to the great Aintree roar that encompassed the gallant winner every year up the long run-in. Pip and Peter, shoving their way back down the steps of the stand, were fighting the tide of euphoria in which they had no part. Their fear and disappointment isolated them from all the grinning, cheering faces that they pushed apart. They were both frightened, not for the fall, but for the stillness out in the country. There were legions of loose horses coming back, but no sign of Dogwood at all

Jonathan got up and immediately fell down again. He could not think why. He tried a second time but a big fat lady in St John's ambulance uniform held him tightly in her arms and said, 'Don't move, dear, you're quite all right here.'

Jonathan swore at her, in spite of her grey hair and kind face, and she said, 'Well, you sound all right,' and let him go.

He had a mouthful of turf, and a large part of him wouldn't move. There did not seem to be any horses coming past, only one lying on its side under the fence which was all smashed above him, the spruce scattered in all directions. It looked familiar, but nothing seemed to connect in Jonathan's brain. He tried to walk towards it, and fell over again. Somebody else got hold of him, and some men went past him towards the horse and bent down over it.

'Steady on, old chap. You went a purler.'

He struggled on all the same, pulling his helpers with him. He could see that the horse was lying quite still, not distorted in any way at all, but as if it was asleep in its field. Its head was stretched out and its eyes were open, but glazed over in a way that Jonathan understood all about. He could not speak. He reached the horse and fell down by its head.

'It's no good, fella,' somebody said, but kindly.

No, he knew it wasn't, but Dogwood wanted him and he wasn't going anywhere else. He put his hand on the warm, steaming neck and stroked the Rolls Royce coat, shining in the bright sunshine. A curious knot of people began to collect, but respectfully, silent. The wind was blowing and the skylarks twittering in shoals after the passing excitement. From the direction of the stands a roar was going up and shreds of the commentary's excitement blew in the sky with the birds, and meant nothing any longer.

'What happened?' Jonathan asked. 'There's nothing

wrong with him.'

'No, lad. He went in mid-air, I was watching. I've seen it before. The old heart....'

The man was undoing Dogwood's girths. 'Makes a nasty fall. But he wouldn't have known.'

Somebody said, 'Here's the vet. He'll tell you.'

Did that make it all right then, Jonathan wondered, that he wouldn't have known? To die in mid-air, doing what he was quite obviously enjoying? Jonathan felt as if he had died in mid-air too, his mind numb. He took Dogwood's bridle off and smoothed his forelock.

The vet, brisk and cheerful, diagnosed heart-attack. 'Not uncommon. Better than a broken leg, old chap.' He clapped Jonathan on the shoulder. 'You were going bloody well too, must have felt bloody marvellous. Owner'll be sick. I'll run you back in my car, if you like. There's nothing you can do here. Get your saddle off.'

They manipulated Jonathan, steering him towards the car, bringing the saddle and bridle, jollying him along. They thought he was concussed and they could well have been right. He was unable to resist, although he wanted to stay. It was all finished and he wanted to stay where it was quiet, out in the country with Dogwood, until he had got things straight in his mind. The wind and the sun were drying Dogwood's sweat and his coat was beginning to stare, his blood was growing cold, and the glaze was fixed over his eyes. Jonathan did not want to leave him.

They made him. The ambulance came up expectantly, its lights flashing, which made Jonathan take the vet's sanctuary, and drive back the way he had galloped so optimistically minutes before. He did not know it, but the tears were running down his cheeks. There was someone in the back with him who put a hand on his shoulder and said, 'I know how it feels. It's happened to me too.'

It was only a horse, after all.

They delivered him to the First Aid department, the crowd parting as the vet held his hand on the horn.

They met up eventually in their own horsebox outside the stables. By then Jonathan had recovered and been cleared by the medicos, washed and changed, and knew that Peter and Pip had never seen him crying. When he came in, Pip said, 'Jonathan!' in a choked voice, and started to cry, but the two boys remained stony-eyed and silent, both of them only too well aware of the abyss, and how best to avoid it. They were as close as they had ever been, united in a stoic inscrutability.

Peter put the kettle on.

Jonathan sat down. He ached everywhere, and parts of him hurt quite badly, nowhere worse than his thinking-areas. He drank strong tea, carefully not thinking, and afterwards they went to Dogwood's empty box and collected all his gear. Horses were coming in from the last race, and a lot of the earlier runners, including most of the National runners, were going out to their horse-boxes, snugly rugged and bandaged and cossetted, their lads relieved and happy now that the tension was over, laughing and shouting goodbye. Trainers, owners and jockeys were taking leave of each other, a good many of the owners obviously well-wined, having either drowned their sorrows or celebrated their wins. Children congregated with their autograph books at the entrance to the car-park, and Jonathan saw the champion jockey, now dressed like a bank manager, stop to sign his name. He hadn't won either, but at least his horse was going home for its tea, to run another day. Surprisingly, quite a few people came over and mumbled some embarrassed words of sympathy, not least a couple of well-known trainers and a television commentator. This, although warming, was hard to acknowledge with the required degree of civil self-control, and it was a relief to retreat back to the living quarters of their meaningless horse-box and stow the rugs, buckets and feed carefully away for the return journey.

'There's not much point staying any longer, is there?' Jonathan enquired.

'Not if you're fit to drive.'

The others were doubtful, but Jonathan relished having his mind occupied with rush-hour driving. The physical pains were nothing like so bad as the bruises in the mind, which the driving might allay. They crowded into the cab and Jonathan edged slowly into the queue of boxes and cars making for the main road. Passing the entrance to the course and seeing the stands and the last of the departing punters Peter came to with a jerk and said, 'Christ, your mother! She said to see her afterwards!'

Jonathan gaped at him, and drove straight into the back of the car ahead. There was a tinkling of smashed lamp-glass and as the irate driver leapt out to assess the damage Jonathan remembered that he was driving without the required licence.

Peter, quick as a flash, leant over and opened the door and said, 'Get out!' He shoved Jonathan out and slipped over into the driving-seat just as one of the traffic policemen came over to see what was going on.

There was the usual argument and waving of arms from the damaged motorist and Jonathan stood back as Peter made the apologies and offered up his licence to the enquiring policeman. The breakages were minimal, tempers cooled, addresses exchanged and the hooting of held-up traffic behind hurried them back into their driving-seats. Under the eye of the policeman Peter had to take the wheel.

'I can't change bloody gear,' he hissed at Jonathan, and they had to go through a farcical two-man driving act to get out on to the main road, Jonathan shoving the gear lever when Peter gave the word, and helping him turn the wheel. By the time they had survived the traffic lights and found somewhere to pull in and change places again, their minds had been refreshingly distracted.

Jonathan, his eyes fixed on the mirror, pulled out into the stream of traffic and said, 'So what about my mother?'

'She was there, said she'd see you in the Members' bar. I

never gave it a thought.'

'I wouldn't have gone anyway.'

Pip said, slowly, 'You ought to tell him the other thing.'

Peter was silent.

'What other thing?'

Peter said, 'He'll drive off the road.'

'Why should I?'

'You've got to tell him,' Pip said.

'She said Iris—you—you've got a daughter.'

Jonathan, having suspected, carefully did not scream or swerve or even gasp. In truth, at that moment he cared far more about Dogwood than any daughter. He cared terribly about Pip knowing. His mother must have told Peter in front of Pip. This last knowledge was as painful as anything that had happened that day.

He made no remark, watching the traffic ahead. The hours of the drive back were the only certain thing in life: after that all the options were bleak in the extreme.

Peter said, into the silence, 'Congratulations and all that.'

He still said nothing and Pip said, 'It can't be all bad. Whatever happened.'

'Can't it?' Did she know, Jonathan wondered? 'What else did she say?'

'Not much. I was rather rude to her,' Peter said. 'And she went away.'

'What are you going to do?' Jonathan asked Peter.

'When we get back? Try and get some more rides until the season's over—another week or so and I'll be fit. Might drop in at home for a day or two.'

Peter was resilient, had knocked his head against brick walls every since childhood. Jonathan envied his instinct for survival. He did not want to think about the future at all, but the present was no consolation.

'Dogwood was fantastic,' he said.

'He might have got a place,' Peter said. 'The second horse fell at the last.'

'He didn't feel tired at all. Not like me. He loved it.'

'He wouldn't have known. Not like breaking a leg. It could have been worse. Even if—I've been thinking about it—his legs were so dicky, there wasn't a great future for him when you think of it. He kept well with us—I think it was probably riding him in the sea, like Red Rum, it made him better. But if he'd gone back to my brother—which is what would have happened—who knows how he'd have ended up?'

'You couldn't retire a horse like Dogwood.'

'No.'

'Not many people want that sort of a hunter. They want horses that don't frighten them.'

'That's right.'

They convinced themselves. But Jonathan remembered the feel of Dogwood, his eagerness and his courage, and knew that nothing could make it right, not all the talk in the world, and a tear collected in the corner of his eye. He screwed it back, not daring to speak any more, and drove grimly down the East Lancashire motorway with the knowledge that there was no solace waiting at the end of the journey, but just more trouble. Trouble all the way.

Chapter 9

The demolition firm turned up at Mallow End the morning after the Grand National and were surprised to find Peter and Jonathan fast asleep in bed.

'What's all this then? You've no right here, you know. We're going to knock this place down.'

'Not today. It's Sunday,' Peter said.

'The men start tomorrow. Eight sharp.'

'Yeah, fine.'

Peter went back to sleep. Jonathan hadn't even woken up.

It was the signal to go, irrevocable. There was a smell of spring and there were primroses on the front lawn where the bulldozers were going to mass for the attack. Jonathan did not want to see it happen.

'You'll have to go home,' Peter said sensibly. 'We can go together, get it over. You can stay at my place if you like, when you've said all the right things—'

'Like what?'

'Oh, hi to your mummy, well done old girl to Iris, nice to meet you to your daughter, that sort of thing. Hasty exit while dust settles.' Peter grinned. 'I'll come too, stand by. I'd like to see it.'

Jonathan smiled too.

'It can't possibly be as bad as you're expecting,' Peter said.

'It can't be worse,' Jonathan said.

They packed up all their gear and put it in a barn at Pip's place, to be collected when convenient. They packed their immediate gear into the motor-bike panniers and Jonathan pulled on his bike leathers, silent. This was the bit he was most dreading, saying goodbye to Pip. What she knew of the business he had no idea, but he had told her nothing. He did not even know if he would get a chance to see her now, away from her parents.

Leaving the place without Dogwood was pretty awful too. They could not help standing in the doorway, looking at his empty quarters, with the spring sun filtering through the cobwebs over the elegant Georgian fanlight. From each other they did not bother to hide their feelings. It was going to hurt for a long time, not just for a day or two, and what might have been would be a question mark for ever.

'He'd have had no life at my brother's,' Peter said. 'Nobody understood him. So all for the best really.'

'If you say so.'

'Even with what happened, I still envy you that ride.'

Well, Jonathan could understand that. He wouldn't forget it. At the moment he certainly couldn't, feeling stiff all over and very bruised about the hips and shoulders. They were two crocks on the motor-bike, progressing at a cautious pace, no backward glances. They had agreed to bid farewell at the farm, a social farewell, to receive condolences and good wishes from Pip's parents. Mrs Anstruther had made coffee and her husband came in from the office and said all the right things. Pip handed round the sugar and cream, very quiet, violet shadows under her eyes. Jonathan scarcely dared look at her. He was feeling desperate again, the parting imminent, and no chance for saying anything. It mattered now. She went into the kitchen to refill the coffee-pot.

Jonathan got up. 'Do you mind if I use your—?'

There was a lavatory outside the kitchen door. He went through, catching Pip's wrist as he went. They went outside and Jonathan pulled the door to. They had the time it takes to fill a coffee-pot. Jonathan pulled Pip close to him and said, 'I do love you,' and bent his head down to kiss her. She put her arms up, her hands cradling his head, and kissed him passionately back. She was half-crying, half-laughing. Jonathan could not pull himself away, dazed by her response, and it was she who freed herself, turning her head away.

'Will you come back? Please, *please*—'

'Yes, yes! Oh, Pip, I'm in such a mess, but I will — I will try.'

'Please, Jonathan! Say you will.'

'Yes, of course I will! But—oh, Christ, I do love you!'

They kissed again, then Pip dragged herself free and reached blindly for the kitchen door. Jonathan stood in an agony of desire, watching her blundering round the coffee-pot, then leaned against the doorpost of the outbuilding, taking deep breaths to bring back sanity. The smell of damp flags and peeling paint, old cobwebs and dead spiders would stay with him forever as mute reminder of this overpowering surge of emotion, his first and only experience of true love— or so he believed. Coming so soon after the Grand National he felt dazed, with good reason. His deep despair and pessimism for the future was now fractured by miraculous gleams of hope. She truly did love him! The feeling of astonished achievement reminded him of landing after Becher's. He groped for the lavatory chain to prove by the flushing of the cistern the innocence of his departure from the coffee circle, and headed back for the living-room. Pip refilled his coffee-cup. He dared not look at her.

Five minutes later they departed. Jonathan rode in a dream, not knowing whether he was elated by what had happened or in despair. Thinking about it, he scarcely noticed his surroundings, driving like a zombie, until he was actually in the back lane of Ravenshall Court, and the particular topography of the ruts struck him by their familiarity. As he rounded the corner of the hay-barn into the stable yard he saw immediately that his mother's car was in its garage. The moment of truth was at hand and he was highly nervous. Perhaps he should leave the engine running...

Peter got off the pillion and unfastened his crash-helmet. He looked anxious too.

'You're sure you want me? I'll wait here if you like.'

'No, mate, you're coming in.'

Jonathan unwound his scarf and was aware of an unexpected pang of sentimental pleasure at being home. Last time he had still been in flight; this time the homecoming was serious, to put the record straight. He had always loved his home, speaking in terms of architecture and geography; its beauty always provided spiritual solace, even if its inhabitants did not. A part of him was feeling pleasure at it even now, when he was expecting no welcome at all.

With Peter close behind he opened the door and went into the stone-flagged passage which led through into the house. The kitchen door was on his left, half open, with washing-machine noises cosily breaking the silence and cups clattering. He went in and his mother, in the act of lifting the coffee percolator off the stove, looked up in surprise.

'Why, Jonathan!'

She was caught off-guard, and her face seemed to break up in—to Peter, the interested spectator—a most unexpected way, momentarily out of control. She almost dropped the percolator back on the stove and came quickly forward and wrapped her arms round Jonathan in an uninhibited embrace.

'Oh, my dear! my dear!'

Peter, somewhat embarrassed, moved round to rescue the coffee which was now boiling all over the stove and caught Jonathan's amazed eyes over his mother's shoulder. Peter winked and Jonathan, surfacing from the shock, put his tongue out. Of all the likely receptions the two of them had pictured, this had never been on the list at all.

Mrs Meredith, true to form, quickly recovered herself, but her relief and joy at seeing Jonathan had been transparent, and there was no way she could cover her tracks.

'You've timed it very well. Fetch two more cups and saucers.... And Peter too! I must say this is very unexpected—I—I—oh dear, I was upset on Saturday—I—I wanted to see you.'

'Well, I didn't know. You're seeing me now,' Jonathan said.

'Peter told you about Iris?'

'Yes.'

'Are you going to stay?'

'It depends.'

'Take your things off. You too, Peter. Sit down.'

They clambered out of their gear, Jonathan so relieved at his welcome that he felt quite giddy. He felt that a week in his own bed would not come amiss; the place was a holiday camp after Mallow End. With luck Iris was away in hospital somewhere....

'I was making a drink for Iris,' his mother said. 'I'll take it up, but I won't tell her you're here, not till you're ready to go up.'

She departed, and Jonathan's optimism went with her, torpedoed by the prospect of meeting Iris again. He could not even think of her without being tormented by his guilt complexes at not loving her. Loving Pip made it worse, pointing up the futility of the affair with Iris.

Peter was grinning. 'Who'd have thought it? She's mellowed since Saturday, that's all I can say. Looks like you're in with a chance.'

His mother came down, smiling. 'The baby is really lovely. You must be very curious to see it?'

'No, I'm not actually.'

'She was born on Thursday, a month premature. But she's so big and strong for eight months they let Iris home after forty-eight hours. They're both doing splendidly.'

'Who is she like?' Peter asked politely, as Jonathan remained conspicuously silent.

'She's fair, like Iris. But not like either of her parents really.'

Jonathan had a wild hope that it might not be his at all—couldn't you have a blood test or something, to find out?—but his mother said, 'She's got Jonathan's nose, quite definitely, and his hands I think. But her hair isn't curly at all and is quite light.'

Jonathan had never seen his mother so tame and dozy. Grandmothering, he thought hopefully, suited her.

'She's so good, hardly cries at all.'

The conversation was so boring both boys found it hard to keep awake. But eventually Mrs Meredith remembered the Grand National and asked Jonathan about his ride. She knew what had happened and had tried to get to him in the medical quarters but they wouldn't let her in.

'I gathered you were only bruised, so I waited for you in the bar as I had told Peter, but I suppose the wretched boy never told you?'

'Yes, he did, but only when we were on our way home. He forgot.'

'It was understandable, I suppose. You must have been very upset.'

At least she knew about things like that, having lost and wept over a horse or two in her life, Jonathan remembered.

'It really is very nice to set eyes on you again, I must say. I'm so glad you decided to come home.'

Jonathan did not dare catch Peter's eye, the brain reeling. No talk of the examinations missed, opportunities let slip, duties undischarged. She actually appeared to love him.

'In some ways, this has been worse than when you were kidnapped,' she said. 'I handled it very badly. Iris told me later about—how she had deceived you. I can't think why you didn't explain at the time.'

Words failed him. While he was still gaping his mother turned to Peter and said, 'And your father will be very pleased to see you again, Peter. He says you're very bad at writing letters and he only knows what you're up to by looking at the racing news. You've been getting a few rides, he says.'

She suggested Jonathan should run Peter home. He could come back and have a bath while she made some lunch. She would ring up his father and tell him the good news.

After all the months of bitterness and hard work and discomfort and uncertainty Jonathan found himself drifting back into the Ravenshall luxury as if in a dream. Wallowing in his mother's approbation, her good cooking, the best bathroom, fishing his old favourite clothes out of mothballed plastic bags, he felt the elegance and comfort of the family riches seeping again into his deprived bloodstream. He was free of work and worry, of ambition and care; he could put his feet up, luxuriate in his mother's kindness, forget all his past troubles. In a day or two it would pall, but the unexpectedness of his situation was bliss. He refused to let the bad memories surface, tried not to think of Pip because he wanted her so badly, put off seeing Iris as long as possible, reflected on his lovely, empty future. His father came home and shook his hand.

'And what do you think of this child of yours? Your mother's gone back twenty years. She's like a cat with the cream—amazing.'

'I haven't seen it yet.'

'You amaze me! It won't go away by your not looking, you know. Not very kind to Iris, surely?'

No, he'd never been very kind to Iris.

'I'll go up.'

It could be deferred no longer. He climbed the stairs slowly and went to Iris's room trying to feel charitable and magnanimous. She was sitting up in bed reading. When she saw him her expression was rather more cautious than joyful, which he found encouraging.

He went and sat on her bed.

'Hi.'

'And to you.'

'Has Mummy told all?'

'Mmm, mostly, I think. She's ever so pleased to have you back.'

'Wonders will never cease.'

'But I'm not especially. It doesn't matter any more.'

Jonathan blinked. 'What doesn't?'

'You not caring about me.'

Jonathan felt like a worm, squirming on a hook. His surprise must have showed, for Iris laughed.

'You ought to be pleased,' she said.

Had he got everything wrong? His mother pleased, Iris not so ... his opinion of their opinions quite reversed. Perhaps he had been concussed after all.

'Pleased? No. I—I never wanted to hurt you. I just want to be free.' It sounded like a line in a bad film.

'You are quite free,' Iris said. 'I've got what I want.'

Jonathan supposed he ought to look at it, and walked round the bed to peer into the cot. Babies honestly all looked alike to him and his own was no different. He was quite curious in a purely biological way to see if, like a good stallion, he stamped his stock, but could see no indications of it, the child looking (if anything) like his mother in one of her better moods. It was quite handsome and well-built, what he could see of it. He tried to feel fond and proud, but could work up nothing at all, save a slightly unworthy wish that the sexier of his companions at school, who were always talking about it, could see that he, without talking about it, had actually produced.

'It's very nice,' he said, politely.

'She.'

'Sorry, she.'

'I'm calling her Anne, if you don't object. Unless you want to call her after your horse.'

'Dogwood?'

'Anne Dogwood Webster. If you want.'

Jonathan considered, wondering if she was joking. He liked the idea. It wasn't pretty, but if it—she—grew up half as good as her namesake they would all be pleased.

'Why not?' To remember him by. He liked his daughter much better already, with that name. He smiled. 'All right, if nobody objects.'

163

'You mother can't object. She told me she christened you after a horse, an old hunter of her father's.'

Lucky it hadn't been called Sunbeam, Jonathan thought, or Highflyer or Lucky Lad.

As neither of them were anxious to ask leading questions like 'What are you going to do?' there did not seem to be much to talk about. There was no common ground in either the Grand National or giving birth, no common ground anywhere in fact, in spite of Anne Dogwood asleep in her cot.

Jonathan, after five minutes' small talk, withdrew. He seemed to have shed a considerable burden, but was still uncertain of his status in regard to Iris. He wondered if he should talk to his father about it, but his father seemed unworried by the additions to his family. He didn't seem unduly worried about Jonathan himself, and nobody mentioned the dread word Meddington, or exams or university, for which Jonathan was deeply grateful.

After two or three days of lying on his bed or in the bath or on the living-room sofa, doing largely nothing at all, Jonathan sought out Peter again. He found Peter lying on the sofa watching 'Playschool' on the television, which he had been doing himself ten minutes earlier.

'Thought I heard the bike,' Peter said. 'How's Daddy then?'

'They're all being terribly nice to me. I can't work it out. How goes it here?'

Peter moved up to make room for Jonathan on the sofa. Peter's brother Giovanni, aged fairly low down in the single figures by Jonathan's estimation, was sitting on the floor, half-watching, half-intrigued with his buggle-gum, which Jonathan hoped to avoid. Peter's home was untidy and comfortable, his Italian step-mother given more to cooking than housework.

'I put on too much weight here,' Peter said. 'I shall have

to go. How's things with you?'

Jonathan told him.

'Iris has gone off me, did you know? I can't believe my luck.'

'She's got someone else.'

'Who said?'

'Oh, hasn't she told you? My ma told me. Gordon Hargreaves.'

'Are you serious?'

'Well, he is, according to ma. She knows his auntie. Gordon dotes on her apparently, little Annie and all.'

Jonathan was astonished yet again. 'Gordon Hargreaves?' The name rung bells in the distant past and conjured up a wet, earnest youth something to do with the Young Conservatives.

'He liked Ruth? That one?'

'Yes. Ruth said he was the sort mothers liked. She preferred the sort they didn't, if you remember.'

'Yes. Poor Ruth.'

He remembered. He felt indignant now, to have been thrown over for a prat like Gordon Hargreaves, and annoyed at feeling indignant, because it was what he wanted, wasn't it? He had said so to Iris in his bad film dialogue.

'Iris hasn't mentioned him.' But Iris had always deceived, if not by not saying, by saying the wrong thing. 'Does my mother know?'

'She must do. He calls properly, in his car, with bunches of flowers and all that crap. No hiding under the bed like some I could mention.'

'You think he might marry her?' And take her away was what he meant, with a great lifting of the heart at the prospect. It was a vision of paradise, Ravenshall empty of Iris. Since she had come to Ravenshall—initially at his own invitation—his home had become untenable. If Iris were to go he could feel he belonged again; his feeling of statelessness, of being a refugee, which had haunted him for the last six months, would dissolve overnight. Splendid Gordon Hargreaves! He could father Anne Dogwood and they could all live happily ever after. Strangely, he now felt a proprietory interest in Anne Dogwood and the thought of Gordon Hargreaves bringing her up depressed him. But he couldn't have it all ways—he certainly didn't want the job. He told Peter about Dogwood being added to the child's name, and Peter was amused.

'I hope she'll thank you for it!' Then, more seriously, 'I hope she's worthy of it.'

'My feelings exactly.'

Jonathan then described his happy state at home, his parents' surprising lack of anxiety for his future, his mother's strange content, his father's tolerance.

'Ive never known them so docile. And just when I was expecting quite the worst.'

'Mine were quite pleased to see me too. Best of all, look—' Peter got up and fetched a letter that was propped on the mantelpiece. He passed it to Jonathan. It was from a well-known trainer asking Peter if he would pay him a visit.

'He wants me to ride for him. He said he likes my "quiet style"—has seen me several times but never actually falling which is a bit of luck. Dad's going to run me over next week when my shoulder will be fit again.'

Jonathan was less surprised than Peter by what Peter thought of as his good luck. He was pleased for Peter, but could not keep his mind from zooming back to the incredible Gordon Hargreaves, and took his leave shortly to go and explore the phenomenon. Of all the simple answers to his problems, the fact that Iris might take a fancy to someone else had never occurred to him. He had accepted the burden of her love for life, like a Sherpa-sized rucksack, and the prospect now of ditching it was euphoric.

When he got home he found his mother in the kitchen preparing a meal. He had been going to confront Iris, but it struck him that he might get the truth from his mother, which was not always a foregone conclusion with Iris. Having all his life avoided heart-to-hearts with his mother, he now found himself unpractised in the approach. He sat on the kitchen table and ate a few raisins out of her ingredients.

'Try and find some decent things to wear tonight. The Hamiltons are coming to dinner,' she said. 'Not jeans.'

'Mmm. Okay.' He wondered what she had told her friends about the new baby upstairs.'

'Have you said—told people—about?'

'Oh, no. Not that you're the father. They might guess but of course nobody would mention it. Fortunately she doesn't look much like you.'

'Peter said that Iris—Iris has got a boy-friend. Gordon Hargreaves, he said.'

'Yes. She met him a few months back. He calls quite often. They seem to like each other.'

'Do you think he wants to marry her?'

Mrs Meredith looked up in astonishment. 'Why? Are you jealous?'

'No. I would like him to. And take her away.'

His mother said, 'I can see that would solve things for you very nicely.'

Jonathan flushed up, feeling angry.

'Yes, it would! I want my home back, and I can't—while she's here. She used me, to get the baby. I'd never have made love to her if she hadn't kept on at me. Now what can I do? I want her to go away.'

His outburst was childish and undignified and put him at a disadvantage ... but being silent and dignified had not helped his case earlier; a diatribe could do no worse.

'She's much too immature to get married. Even if Gordon wants it I would not agree to it, I'm afraid. I could not forbid her, of course, but I'm sure I could dissuade her.'

'If they both want it?'

'Yes. Considering it's your baby's future that is at stake,

I would have thought you could see my point. Gordon for all his virtues, is a very unimaginative young man and would find Iris very hard going. I would certainly ask them to think very hard, and wait for a considerable time before committing themselves.'

'Anybody's going to find Iris hard work.'

'True. All the more reason to guide her.'

And what is my position, all the while she's here?' Jonathan spoke bitterly.

'Your position is what you've made it, my dear. You are the father of her child whether you like it or not. Other young men get caught in just the same way—it's nothing new—and take on the financial responsibility, the whole responsibility, if the girl has no one to fall back on. Some don't, admitted, but many do. At least you haven't got that. But you still have the moral responsibility.'

His mother's implacable reasoning goaded Jonathan.

'You like this situation! You like being a grandmother, don't you? That's why you want to keep Iris here.'

'Yes, I do.'

She was different, no longer driving and assertive, but calm and domestic. She was not even angry with him any more. She seemed to have lost her burning ambition for his future and transferred her interest to Iris and the new member of the family. It should have made things easier for him, but somehow it didn't. He was confused, and wondered if there was a perversity in him which always wanted the thing he hadn't got.

'Then what is my position?' he asked again. 'What am I to do?'

She had always told him in the past and he had resented it. Now he was lost.

'You do what you like, Jonathan,' she said.

'About everything? University—a job, Iris and everything?'

'Yes. You must make your own decisions.'

He had never been offered such freedom before. He got

off the table, took another handful of raisins and went slowly upstairs. He went back to Iris. She was feeding the baby, sitting in the window looking out over the front lawns. He went across and offered her a raisin. She nibbled it off his hand, like a horse, over the baby's head and Jonathan felt the baby's soft hair on the back of his outstretched hand.

His mother had just given him the freedom of the universe, but there was no such thing. For the first time the baby stirred him.

'What's wrong?' Iris asked.

'Nothing, I suppose.'

'I told you—not to worry about me any more. I shall go away soon.'

'Where will you go?'

'I shall go home when my mother comes back. I might get married.'

'To Gordon Hargreaves?'

She laughed. 'Would you mind? It's your baby, to be given a father, after all.'

'No. I've no right to. But don't marry Gordon just to make things proper. Not if you don't really like—love—him.' He could scarcely believe he was saying it. His whole being longed for her to marry Gordon Hargreaves, to rub out his account, square his life's path.

'I might love him in time. I certainly don't love anyone else.'

And she looked him right in the eye in a very strange way, fiercely. Her eyes were green like Pip's, he noticed with a pang, but yellower and eaglish. They made him feel terrible.

'I'm fed up with your family, fussing,' she said belligerently. 'And you. I want to go away.'

Jonathan got up from his seat on the bed, as amazed by the girl as ever.

'Fine,' he said. 'Suits me.'

He went out of the room and downstairs, out into the

garden. The daffodils were just starting, the great yellow seas that the public paid to come and look at on Sundays. He walked through them, unseeing. If he had got things right—and it was difficult—he thought that he was a free man. He was free to go back to Pip, free to work out what he wanted to do with his life, free of Oxford. It took a bit of getting used to, such largesse.

He walked on, hands in pockets, bemused. The air smelled of spring and the year's beginning, the season for fresh starts. The idea was taking hold. Another hundred yards or so of daffodils, he reckoned, and he would come to terms with it.

Iris watched him from the window. Jonathan, being so honest himself, always believed her lies, and he had believed the biggest whopper of the lot, about her not loving him any more. She watched him possessively, knowing that, through the child, she had a life's hold on him. She told herself fiercely that she would never use it, because she loved him too much, but sometimes she did not have the strength to do the right thing—it had been proved in the past.

She thought she was improving, because all her lies in the past had been to help her own cause, not somebody else's. They said she was growing up, becoming more responsible. She hoped very much it was true, but a leopard could not change its spots and not even time could make her what she knew she wasn't.

'I will do my best,' she said to the baby. 'You must help me, not to love your daddy.'

She watched Jonathan till he disappeared out of sight into the lime avenue, by which time she was crying, and it was time to get dressed and go downstairs.

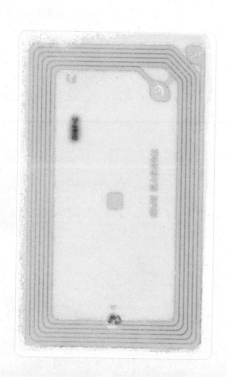